Amigas
She's Got Game!

Amigas

She's Got Game

by Veronica Chambers

Created by Jane Startz
Inspired by Jennifer Lopez

Hyperion
New York

Copyright © 2010 Jane Startz Productions and Nuyorican Productions

All rights reserved. Published by Hyperion, an imprint of Disney Book Group.
No part of this book may be reproduced or transmitted in any form or by any
means, electronic or mechanical, including photocopying, recording, or by
any information storage and retrieval system, without written permission
from the publisher. For information address Hyperion,
114 Fifth Avenue, New York, New York 10011-5690.

Printed in the United States of America
First Edition
1 3 5 7 9 10 8 6 4 2

J689-1817-1-10182

Library of Congress Cataloging-in-Publication Data on file

ISBN 978-1-4231-2364-4

Designed by Jennifer Jackman

Visit www.hyperionteens.com

For my chambelán, Jason
—V.C.

*To my wonderful family—Peter, Jesse, Kate,
and Zoë, who are always my inspiration. I'm so
lucky to be surrounded by such a wise, funny, and
caring group of friends and loved ones.*
—J.S.

CHAPTER 1

ALICIA CRUZ, one of the founding members of Amigas Incorporated, giggled nervously as she boarded a boat moored to one of the more exclusive docks in Miami. Following close behind were her two best friends, Carmen Ramirez-Ruben and Jamie Sosa. They quickly mimicked her unusually high-pitched laugh. Shooting them a disapproving look, Alicia tried to regain her composure. After all, this wasn't just an ordinary hanging-out-with-her-friends kind of Saturday; they had a business to run.

It was the past summer when Alicia, Carmen, Jamie, and Alicia's boyfriend, Gaz, had started a business planning *quinceañeras*, or Sweet Fifteen parties. And even though the friends were only teenagers themselves, they'd quickly become the hottest game in town.

They knew how to make a celebration that was modern but respectful of tradition; innovative; and, most important, not corny. A *quince* was like a wedding, debutante ball, and graduation all rolled into one, and Amigas Inc. had perfected the art of making their *quinces* rock. Still, no matter how many they planned, there were bound to be surprises. And certainly, when they had woken up that morning, none of them had imagined that they'd be taking a private ferry to the Mortimer family estate.

Growing up in Miami pretty much provided assurance that by the time you reached high school you'd have been on or around every type of boat, pontoon, and Jet Ski there was. What made the Mortimers' boat—the *Santa Maria* was the name scrawled across the side—different was that literally everything on it smelled of money, from the polished oak floors to the shiny brass flagpole to the gold-stitched, monogrammed life jackets. Coral Gables had its share of rich kids, including Alicia Cruz. But Binky Mortimer and her golf-champ brother, Dash, were on a whole other level. And everything about the family ferry, which in any other part of the world would have been called a yacht, confirmed the fact that this was not the kind of wealth you encountered every day. Nor, Alicia suspected, was their destination the kind you encountered every day.

Miami was surrounded by dozens of small islands.

The most famous of these was Fisher Island, where Oprah Winfrey had a house. But even Oprah lived on an island with other people. The Mortimers, as far as the girls knew, were the only family in Miami to live on their *own* island.

Knowing all that (from living in Miami and reading the daily gossip blogs), it was not a stretch to say that Alicia had been surprised—no, make that floored—when she received an e-mail from *the* Binky Mortimer early in the morning saying that she wanted to hire Amigas for her *quinceañera*. It had read:

> Yo-delay-lihoo. I'm having a *quince*, and it's going to be hotter than the three-pepper special at Taco Bell. I hear Amigas Inc. is the only gig in town that can pull this throwdown off. So, as Donald Trump would say, "You're hired." Come to my island at 3 p.m. for a meeting. XO, XO, Binky.

Alicia knew that saying no was out of the question. She had quickly told the rest of the group and asked if they were up for a meeting after school. Their reactions had varied. Carmen had flipped at the idea. Jamie had rolled her eyes and said something about "another snobby sitch in the making." And Gaz? Well, he had just asked, "Who?" Apparently, he did not read the Miami social pages, and perhaps, Alicia had joked, he lived under a rock.

Now, standing on the deck of the Mortimers' private ferry, the conversation returned to the most popular topic since they had agreed to meet Binky. Alicia and her girls were of decidedly different minds about whether a non-Latin girl could or *should* have a *quince*. Carmen, who'd just thrown an "Hola, Shalom!" *quince* that celebrated her Latino heritage and Jewish religion, was all for it.

"Being Latin is all about being inclusive," Carmen said. "Our people represent practically every skin color and dozens of nationalities. We're a *global* culture."

Carmen was nearly six feet tall and had flawless *café con leche*–colored skin. Her dark hair fell in waves down her shoulders. She looked like a model, but designing clothes was her passion. She was dressed for the Mortimer meeting in a Carmen original, a hot pink one-shouldered blouse with a pair of wide-legged khaki pants.

Alicia nodded in agreement. But her mind was more on the money than on the culture. "Do you know how much we could make planning a Mortimer party? Money is no object for Binky Mortimer, people. This will take Amigas Incorporated to the next level."

Her eyes sparkled as the headlines and gossip-blog

postings flashed through her mind. Alicia's drive for success was hereditary. She was the daughter of Marisol and Enrique Cruz, who made up one of Miami's power couples. Her mom was a judge, and her dad was the deputy mayor. Alicia had an engaging smile, cascading curls, and a flair for vintage style, aided by the fact that her mom had one of those huge walk-in closets like Carrie Bradshaw's in *Sex and the City*. Today she was dressed in an original DVF leopard-print wrap dress and a pair of Forever 21 pumps. Her goal? To look like the head *chica* in charge.

Though Carmen and Alicia had been pals since elementary school, Jamie had only joined the posse at the end of junior high. Her skin was naturally bronze, with a tan that was the envy of South Beach, and she had dark, stick-straight hair. Jamie had the graceful build of a dancer and the don't-mess-with-me attitude of a prizefighter. It was an unusual combination, but on Jamie, it worked. She was from the Bronx, and while her attempts to "keep it real" could sometimes be a real pain in the butt, Jamie succeeded at them. She was the third Musketeer. Without her, they would just have been your run-of-the-mill "besties."

The sole male member of Amigas Inc. was Gaz (short for Gaspar) Colón. Gaz was a promising musician and an all-around great guy. Gaz's father had died when he was young. To help supplement the modest income his mother made as a cleaning woman, Gaz worked part-time, after school and on weekends, at the Gap. This added responsibility made the amount of time he could spend with Amigas Inc. somewhat limited. But he did what he could.

He and Alicia had met in the sixth grade, when Alicia had enlisted him to play in her newly formed ska band. The band was short-lived, but their friendship was not. After many years of being buddies, followed by a brief "flirtationship," they finally admitted that their feelings had blossomed into something greater, more akin to love. Now they were officially together, and Alicia felt a familiar fluttery feeling as she thought about him. She just wished he could be there now, and not at the Gap, so that he could experience all of this with her and the rest of the group.

Suddenly a crew member in a crisp white shirt and black bow tie approached, cutting into Alicia's thoughts and interrupting the *quince*-or-not-to-*quince* debate. In a faint British accent, he offered them "a refreshment," and held up a silver tray with three sodas, three glasses of ice, a dish of lemon wedges, and a small silver bowl of bananas.

"Wow, thanks," Alicia said, taking the glass that was handed to her and resisting the urge to call the man Jeeves.

"This is nuts," Carmen whispered. "It's a fifteen-minute boat ride and they offer snacks." Jamie either was unimpressed or didn't care about the serious fabulosity of their boat ride. She had resumed her monologue outlining her issues with the idea of Binky's *quince*. "You let white guys rap and you end up with more Vanilla Ices than Eminems. You let *gringas* have *quinces* and next thing you know, Miley Cyrus will be recording in Spanish and winning all the Latin Grammys. *Algunas cosas deben pertenecer sólo a nosotras*. Some things should be just for us."

Alicia and Carmen stifled giggles. They had been hearing this nonstop since they'd made their decision to meet with the client. But they were now on the boat, and nothing could be done to avoid the meeting. "Let's hold off on the judging till we actually meet Binky, 'kay, Jamie?" Alicia said, a teasing tone in her voice.

Jamie shrugged. "Fine, whatever. I'm just saying."

"We know, we know. Just for us. Got it," Carmen said, laughing.

The waves parted as the ferry slowed on its approach to the Mortimers' home. The girls stopped debating for a moment to take in the turquoise blue waters, the lush green landscape of palm trees that shimmered before them, and . . . the two cute boys in kayaks who paddled past them.

"*Hola*, beautiful ladies!" one of the guys called out, causing the girls to blush. His T-shirt said UNIVERSITY OF MIAMI. Even though Carmen and Alicia had boyfriends, they both smiled and waved.

"Which one of you lovely ladies is single?" the second boy in the kayak called out. He had curly blond hair, and he, too, was wearing a U. of Miami T-shirt.

"She is!" Alicia and Carmen called out in unison, pointing to Jamie and cracking up.

"What's your phone number, single girl?" the boy called out. "I've got a photographic memory."

"It doesn't take a photographic memory to memorize a seven-digit number," Jamie called back. "Looks like you're not smart enough to date me."

The boy looked wounded and mimed being shot in the heart. His friend said something they couldn't hear, and then the boys waved and paddled away.

"He was cute," Carmen said, as the girls flopped down on the comfortable seats that lined the deck. "You should have given him your number. Like you gave Domingo mine." She smiled as she thought about her supercute boyfriend, whom she'd met while planning her own *quince* in October. They'd been pretty much inseparable ever since, and she owed it all to Jamie, who had snuck him her number when she wasn't looking.

As far as Carmen and Alicia knew, their friend had never had a serious boyfriend in Florida, which seemed nothing short of inconceivable, given the fact that Jamie was both sharp-witted and absolutely gorgeous. But she always compared the guys at Coral Gables High to the guys back in New York, and inevitably, the South Florida guys fell short. Jamie always said they were "corny" or "adolescent" or "sheltered."

The guys in the kayak, however, as her friends would have pointed out, seemed anything but.

"You know what? I'm just going to scream out your phone number," Alicia said, grabbing Jamie's arm.

"Do it, Alicia!" Carmen urged. "Who knows, Jamie? She could be setting you up with the man of your dreams."

"Yeah, picture me dating some guy I met as he paddled by me in a kayak," Jamie said.

"Don't girls date guys they meet on the subway in New York?" Alicia asked.

"All the time," Jamie answered. "There are mad sexy boys on the six train. Holla."

"So, it's the same thing. In New York, you roll on subways. In Miami, we roll on boats," Alicia observed.

"Point taken," Jamie said, shrugging. "Still, I'll pass."

"Except for the fact that unless you count my parents' broken-down rowboat, we don't 'roll' on boats," Carmen pointed out. "We don't live *La Vida* Yacht Club."

"We don't," Alicia said. "But she does." The girls looked in the direction of Alicia's gaze. They had arrived at the dock. And bouncing down the white wooden staircase towards the elaborate yellow and white dock (complete with latticework, gazebo, and orchid-festooned archway) was a girl who could only have been Binky Mortimer. She was tall—almost as tall as Carmen, which put her at a cool five feet eight inches at least. She had platinum blond hair that fell, Gwen Stefani style, in loose waves around her shoulders. Her dark blue eyes were framed in dark liner, and her lip gloss was a classic Palm Beach coral. Dressed in Pucci from head to toe, Binky was wearing a hot pink, black, and white halter dress, a matching turban, and sky-high hot pink heels. "Yoo-hoo, I'm here! I'm coming, ladies. Don't fret!"

"Don't fret?" Jamie repeated, rolling her eyes. "She's acting like we just arrived in the hood at two a.m. during a blackout, instead of pulling up to Moneyville in broad daylight."

"I'm on my way!" Binky called. In her excitement, she tripped on the last step and broke her heel.

"Stupid shoes," she said, tossing them aside and continuing toward them barefoot.

"Did you see what she just did?" Jamie whispered to Carmen.

"Broke a heel?" Carmen asked.

"Broke a very expensive heel, more like it," Alicia chimed in.

Jamie nodded. "Those were vintage Jimmy Choos, Resort Collection 2007."

Jamie was the artist in the group, and one of her many projects was a collection of hand-painted graffiti sneakers that she sold online. Jamie knew everything there was to know about shoes, especially vintage. And while kicks were her specialty, she was also the resident expert on all things Manolo, Choo, and Louboutin.

"Only five hundred pairs of those shoes were made," Jamie sighed. "Those go for about eighteen hundred dollars on eBay."

"She probably took them out of her mom's closet," Alicia said, guessing from her own experience. As they made their way off the boat, she added in a whisper, "I bet she has no idea how much they cost."

Oblivious of the scrutiny, Binky rushed up to the

amigas and promptly gave them each a big hug. "I just know we're going to be besties," she said, grinning broadly.

The girls were a little surprised by the heavy-duty PDA from their newest client. Alicia and Carmen went with it, hugging Binky back. But Jamie remained reserved.

"Bummer about your shoe," she said instead.

"No big whoop." Binky shrugged. "I'll just get another pair."

Sensing that Jamie was about to lose it with their client, Alicia looped her arm through Jamie's and led her toward the dock's steps.

"Stay cool, Sosa," Alicia whispered. "Remember, the client is always right."

Jamie began to mutter in Spanglish. "*Esta tipa rica* makes me *completamente* nuts. *La más abusadora de todas las abusadoras.*"

Ignoring her friend, Alicia turned around to see that Carmen had calmly and deftly swooped the Choos out of the trash can where they'd been dumped.

"You know, *chica*, these can be fixed," Carmen said to Binky. "Any good shoe-repair shop can make these just like new."

"Really?" Binky said, as though this were the craziest

thing she'd ever heard. "That's a great idea. I'm always breaking a heel. I'm such a klutz. It never occurred to me to try to fix them. My stepmother told me to just throw them away. But I will fix those broken shoes, and then I will donate them to charity."

"Or you could wear them again, after they are fixed," Carmen pointed out. Recycling and resourcefulness were a necessary part of Carmen's life. She had four sisters, a brother, a stepfather, and a stepmother who was a *telenovela* star. That meant a lot of personalities, a lot of clothes, a lot of sharing, and a lot of patience—all of which made Carmen a huge asset to Amigas Inc. and a great friend.

"Let's not go crazy," Binky said. "No need for me to wear broken shoes when I can use them to help save the world by giving them to poor people. Speaking of which, what size are you?"

"I'm a size seven," Carmen said.

"Great! Me, too! If you can fix these, you can have them," Binky said.

"Really?" Carmen asked. Unlike Jamie, she wasn't easily offended. "I'd love them."

"But only if you promise me that you won't go to a bad neighborhood to get them repaired," Binky added. "I wouldn't want you risking your life over a pair of shoes. I can always make Manuel, the butler, do it. He was in the army in Nicaragua and has mad combat skills."

"There's a shoe-repair shop right down the street from my house," Carmen said, trying not to burst out laughing at Binky's warped perception of reality. "I think I'll be fine."

When the *amigas* and Binky reached the top of the dock stairs, the house still loomed ahead, a good five-minute walk from where they stood. No wonder Binky had broken a heel, Carmen thought. There was a lot of walking to do around here. The grounds were elaborately laid. From where they stood, they could make out a tennis court, fountains, and a pool, with what looked like marble steps.

"Let's go to the north pool area," Binky said. "Estrella will bring us lunch out there."

"The north pool?" Alicia asked. "Is there a south pool as well?"

Binky nodded. "The north pool is saltwater, and the south pool is freshwater, of course," she said.

"Of course," Jamie muttered, rolling her eyes.

Alicia nudged her with her elbow and then, turning, followed Binky.

CHAPTER 2

AT THE POOL, Binky turned and shot them all what they were quickly learning was her trademark megawatt smile. "I'm so happy you all decided to come and spend the day with me. We don't get nearly enough visitors at Isla de la Luz."

"Isla de la Luz?" Carmen asked. "Why do you call it that?"

"My father named it after my mother, Luz Yadira Camila Sanchez de la Vega," Binky said. "She was from Venezuela and was the most beautiful woman in Miami. She died when I was just a baby. Breast cancer. Which just sucks. Orange is my favorite color, but I always wear something pink to honor her."

"So, you're half Latina?" Alicia asked, looking over at Jamie and raising an eyebrow.

"Yeah, isn't that cool?" Binky said. "My father's family sailed over on the *Mayflower*. My mother's family is still in Venezuela. Dash, my brother, and I go to visit them every summer. But he was older when my mother passed. She only spoke Spanish to him, so his accent is really, really good. My accent, not so much."

"I'm mixed, too," Carmen said. "My mother is from Mexico and my father is Jewish and Argentinean."

"Oh, my gosh! We're like sisters!" Binky cried, giving Carmen another big hug.

"What's with all the hugging?" Jamie whispered to Alicia. "It makes me want to . . ."—she leaned over and mimed throwing up near a bush of brightly colored plumeria. Alicia shot her a look. It was too late. Binky had clearly seen, and the sadness flashed across her face. Quickly, though, she was back to her cheerful self. "As I was saying, I'm really glad to have you guys here," she went on. "My brother's away a lot at golf tournaments, and my father's always at work. If it weren't for Estrella, our housekeeper, I'd be stranded on this island with just my stepmother all the time."

"I take it that means the evil stepmother thing has some truth to it?" Alicia asked.

Binky shrugged. "I don't know if *evil* is the word. It's more like she's very, very . . . cold. For example, she told my father she would prefer it if I didn't hug her except on holidays and special occasions."

The girls traded looks of disbelief.

"That's *nuts*. It can't be true," Carmen said.

Binky looked as if she'd revealed too much and changed the subject. "Do you guys want to have our big planning meeting in the Jacuzzi?"

"We didn't bring our suits," Jamie pointed out.

"*No problema, amigas,*" Binky said, in what was possibly the worst Spanish accent the friends had ever heard. "There are tons of suits in the changing rooms." She pointed across the pool. At every corner there was a blue-and-white-striped cabana, like a small circus tent.

"I'm down," Alicia said, taking off for a changing room. "I love a Jacuzzi."

"Me, too," said Carmen. "I'll come with you."

Jamie looked at her friends, who were smiling just a little wickedly at her obvious misery. This simply solidified in her mind why they *shouldn't* have been there.

"Fine," Jamie groaned. "Fine."

"Great," Binky said. "Meet you back here in ten!"

The *tres amigas* piled into a cabana together. As each of them looked around, it was hard not to be impressed. This was no simple changing room. It had a full-length mirror in an elaborate gold frame, a rack of bathing suits for men and women, a chaise longue covered in the same striped fabric as had been used on the cabana, and a small refrigerator with sodas and minibottles of champagne.

"Since when do we do business meetings in a Jacuzzi?" Jamie asked, grumpily. "It's totally unprofessional."

"Maybe," Alicia said. "But I have a feeling that this isn't going to be our run-of-the-mill *quinceañera.*"

"You can say that again. Nothing about Binky Mortimer is run-of-the-mill," Carmen agreed. "Hey, check this out. All of the suits are brand-new. They still have their tags on them."

"Oooh, I like this one!" Alicia exclaimed, grabbing a white suit with side cutouts.

"So, Binky's mom is Latina," Carmen said, stepping behind a curtain and pulling on a simple two-piece. "Who knew she was a secret Latina at large?"

"It takes more than having a Latin mom to be a true Latina," Jamie said, grabbing the nearest swimsuit and pulling it on in a huff.

"Really? What does it take?" Carmen asked, needling her friend.

"It takes *flava,*" Jamie said defiantly.

Alicia and Carmen guffawed.

"You mean those dollar-ninety-nine packets of flava?" Alicia asked.

"I mean the born-in-the-barrio, money-can't-buy-it flava," Jamie tossed over her shoulder as she made her way back out into the sunshine.

As they walked to the Jacuzzi, Carmen asked Alicia, "Were you born in the barrio?"

"Nope," Alicia answered, smiling.

"Me, neither," Carmen said. "So, where'd we get our flava?"

"I think Queen Jamie anointed us with it," Alicia whispered.

"That must be it. I hereby pronounce you Lady Alicia of the Barrio, numero uno Cubana Americana business mogul of the kingdom," Carmen declared, pantomiming tapping Alicia on the shoulder with a scepter.

"And I hereby pronounce you Dame Carmen, cultural beacon of Latina fashion and design," Alicia replied. Carmen bowed slightly.

Jamie, who had been pretending to ignore them, laughed in spite of herself. "You know I can hear you, right?" she said.

"We were just making a point. Be nice to our new friend," Alicia said. "She seems like a sweet girl."

"New *client*, not new *friend*," Jamie said. "Big difference. And sweet? Well, so is a piece of sour candy—until you bite into it."

CHAPTER 3

WHILE THEY'D been changing, Estrella, the Mortimer's maid, had brought out a pitcher of iced hibiscus tea, accompanied by a monogrammed silver platter holding a collection of little sandwiches with the crusts cut off. Although the *amigas* had enjoyed a collective eye roll when Binky exclaimed, "Watercress and cucumber, my favorite!" they had to admit that the sandwiches were pretty delicious. They nibbled on a few before heading into the Jacuzzi.

"So, I guess the first question is, when's your birthday?" Carmen asked when they were in the water.

"December first," Binky replied. "So I'm hoping to have my *quince* the Saturday after Thanksgiving."

"That's just over four weeks away!" Jamie cried. "And it's totally not *quince* season. It will end up blending into the holidays. Maybe you should wait until the spring?"

"No way," Binky said, shaking her head. "I really want to have my *quince* next month, near my actual birthday."

"Well we've got a Thanksgiving break in there," Alicia said, her mind racing. "That'll give us a little more time toward the end of planning. But we would still need to start right away."

Carmen nodded. "We should probably contact a church for the ceremony. Are you a member anywhere?" she asked.

"Our Lady of Big Bucks," Jamie whispered to Alicia, who quickly shushed her.

"Our family has been going to the Cathedral of San Miguel since I was a little baby," Binky said. "My brother likes to go to the Spanish services to keep up his vocabulary."

"Well, we have to contact the priest right away to make sure they don't have another *quinceañera* booked," Alicia said. "This wouldn't be the first time that we had to change churches because another *quince* got there first. Miami is crazy like that."

As they talked, the girls had gotten out of the Jacuzzi to avoid getting pruney. Now, Binky was lying on a chaise longue, eating from a bowl of frozen grapes. "Change churches? Are you kidding me? My father is friends with the Pope. My *quince will* be at the cathedral, and if someone else is there, they will find another alternative."

Alicia and Carmen exchanged glances, thinking the same thing. How could Binky be so sweet one moment and so diva the next?

"O-*kay*, then. Well, that still leaves your theme," Alicia said, moving on.

This seemed to worry Binky. "Can I think it over and get back to you with some thoughts? I've just got so much going on in my life right now, I really need to chew on that one for a while," she said.

"I guess it's okay if you aren't set on your theme yet. But we need to know sooner rather than later. It's going to impact your outfit choices. I'm going to need at least two weeks to make your dress," Carmen replied.

"And teach your *damas* and *chambelanes* the dances," Jamie added.

"*Da*-what and *chambe*-who?" Binky asked.

Jamie tried hard not to groan, roll her eyes, or hit her forehead. "*Damas* and *chambelanes*," she repeated. "It means 'ladies and gentlemen.' You have to have seven girls and seven guys. They make up your court. Along with you, it makes fifteen. Get it? Have you even been to a *quinceañera* before?"

"A few," said Binky, clueless as to the extent of Jamie's scorn. "But that's why I'm hiring you guys. I want you to teach me everything there is to know about being a Latina."

"Can't your Latina maid help?" Jamie asked in a sarcastic tone.

"Actually, it was Estrella's idea that I have a *quinceañera*," Binky said, once again not picking up on Jamie's tone. "She said my mother would have loved it. Estrella used to work for my mom, and she always says that the last thing my mother told her before she died was, 'Take care of my little girl.'"

At the mention of Binky's mother, Jamie softened. "How old were you when she passed away?"

"Eighteen months," Binky said.

"So, you don't remember anything about her?" Jamie asked.

"Not a thing," Binky said. "But I always tell people, don't be fooled by the blond hair and blue eyes; I'm proud of my Latina heritage."

Jamie took a deep breath. It was obvious that she wasn't sure what to make of Binky. She was about to ask how Binky could be proud of her Hispanic heritage when she didn't know anything about it when two guys—two oddly familiar guys—approached.

"Hey, I recognize you," the blond one said. "The lovely ladies from the *Santa Maria.*"

"Knock it off, Troy," Binky warned, laughing. She stood up and pointed to the quiet one with the dark hair and impossibly long eyelashes. "*Chicas,* this is my brother, Dash Mortimer. And this piece of country-club vermin is his best friend, Troy Haviland."

Binky punched Troy in the arm. From the way she teased him about his upper-crust status, it seemed suddenly clear that she didn't take the whole richer-than-God thing that seriously—at least all the time.

"Enchanted," Troy said, kissing the hand of each of the girls.

"*Encantado,*" Dash said, bowing.

"Oh, yes, the Spanish-speaking member of the Mortimer family," Jamie said, with a faint tinge of sass in her voice, although both Alicia and Carmen could also hear a quaver. They exchanged glances. Jamie *never* quavered around guys.

"*Sí ¿y usted? ¿Hablas español?*" Dash asked, sitting next to Jamie. He looked deep into her eyes, as if she and he were the only two people in the entire world.

Jamie, whose Spanish-language skills were limited, felt herself flush and scooted her towel away from him.

It was unnerving to have someone look so closely at one, as though they could read one's soul. "It doesn't matter if I speak it or not," she said, answering him in English. "I'm one hundred percent Latina."

"What you are," Dash said flirtatiously, "is one hundred percent beautiful."

Jamie flushed deeper and looked away.

"So, you girls are helping my sister with her *quinceañera*, right?" Dash asked, taking his eyes off Jamie for just a moment. He quickly turned back. "Do you need a *chambelán* to escort you to Binky's *quince*?"

Jamie shook her head, trying to slow her suddenly racing heart. "Only the girls in the court need a *chambelán*."

Dash winked. "Oh, I don't know about that. A girl as beautiful as you should always have a *chambelán* to do your bidding."

"You want to do my bidding?" Jamie asked. She was about to say something flirty, funny, maybe a little saucy, because for a moment she really had forgotten that they were surrounded by other people. Until—

"What he wants to do is ask you out, but he's too corny to say so right out," Troy interjected.

Jamie's face turned red, and she tried to get back on course. She made a halfhearted attempt to turn toward

Alicia and engage in conversation with her. But Dash was having none of that.

He pulled Jamie up from her seat and away from the other loungers. "Sorry to take you away," he whispered, "but Troy is right. I would like to ask you out. So, um, would it be cool if maybe I—um—called you sometime?" His eyes were hopeful and, Jamie couldn't help noticing, adorable.

"You could," she said, "but you can't if I don't give you my number." She didn't understand where this new flirtatiousness was coming from, but she didn't really care. She hadn't felt this way in ages, and she had to admit she didn't want the feeling to go away.

"Well, *could* I have your number?" Dash asked.

"No," Jamie said, shaking her head. "Not yet."

"Discúlpame, no entiendo inglés," Dash said, smiling and pretending not to understand English. He was good-looking and clearly romantic, but more than that, he had a kind of easy confidence. His friend Troy seemed like a junior varsity Romeo by comparison.

Binky suddenly stood up and came over to them. "I hate to break up your tête-à-tête, but this meeting is actually about me and my *quinceañera*."

Dash turned away from Jamie and gave Binky a hug. "You're right, sis. Mom would be so proud of you right now. Besides, I should get to golf practice. You coming, Troy?"

"Yeah, reluctantly." Troy stood up and blew kisses at Alicia and Carmen. "One of you girls is going to be the future Mrs. Troy Haviland."

Carmen and Alicia guffawed at his audacity.

"Oh, yeah? Which one?" Alicia asked.

"Doesn't matter which one," Troy said. "You're both gorgeous."

"I feel so special right now—not," Carmen said, shaking her head.

"Nice meeting you, Alicia and Carmen," Dash said with sincerity. Then he turned to Jamie. "You'll find that I don't scare easily."

"Yeah, yeah, you got mad game," Jamie said, waving him away. But the smile on her face suggested she wanted anything but for him to go away.

She watched him leave with a mixture of interest and frustration. He was cute, but so what? Clearly, he knew it, which made him automatically less cute. But then again, he also seemed smart, which *was* totally cute. She was in such a daze that she didn't hear Alicia calling her.

"Jamie? Hello, Jamie?" Alicia said. "Time to go. We're going to brainstorm some more about themes for

Binky." Turning, she said to their new client, "And you'll meet us tomorrow afternoon at my house to give us your ideas and hammer out a plan. Sound good?"

Binky nodded.

"Works for me," Jamie said absently.

Binky then walked the girls down to the dock and gave them each a bear hug. "This is the most fun I've had in, like, forever," she said. "I can't wait until tomorrow! How do you say good-bye in Latina?"

"Umm, we usually just say adios," Alicia said.

"I was just kidding!" Binky laughed. "I'm blond, but not a dumb blond. Adios! Adios! Adios!"

She gave them all gigantic hugs once again and ran back up the dock, disappearing from view.

CHAPTER 4

"SO, WHAT DO you think?" Carmen asked on the ride back to reality.

"She's friendlier than I would've thought," Alicia said.

"She's not friendly, she's fake," Jamie countered. The fresh air and salt water had cleared her mind of Dash—mostly—and she was back on her anti-Binky bent. "And she's used to buying her friends."

"I dunno," Carmen said. "I get the feeling that Binky's the sort of girl who knows a lot of people, but doesn't necessarily have a ton of close friends."

"Me, too," Alicia concurred.

"Well, asking people, 'How do you say good-bye in Latina?' is not the way to make friends," Jamie said, clearly bothered. "It's, like, hello, Einstein, 'Latina' isn't a language."

"She was just joking," Carmen said.

"Are you so sure of that?" Jamie asked.

There was a moment of silence as all three girls stared into the distance. The sun was setting, and the Mortimer island receded into the distance like a picture on a postcard or in a travel magazine. The air was sultry—the classic Miami mix of hot and humid—and the waters of Biscayne Bay glistened, emerald and aquamarine.

"I feel like I'm in a movie," Alicia and Carmen said at the same time.

They both began giggling. "Jinx!" Alicia said.

"You owe me a Coke," Carmen said.

Five seconds later, as if by magic, the waiter appeared with his silver tray. "Excuse me, ladies, did somebody ask for a Coke?"

They burst out laughing, happily accepting the cold drinks.

"Okay," Alicia said. "Change of topic: how much was Binky's brother crushing on you, Jamie?"

Jamie tried to deny it. "It's not even like that. . . ." she began. But her face was getting hot, because she knew that the flirting had gone more than one way. In spite of herself, she found she liked him. Or at least, she hadn't been able to stop thinking about him since he'd walked away. But she'd gone down that route before—falling for a spoiled rich boy in New York—and it hadn't ended well.

Fool me once, shame on you. Fool me twice, shame on me, she thought now.

It was best she played it cool.

"He was totally and completely into you; it was, like, love at first sight," Carmen said.

"There's no such thing as love at first sight," Jamie said, determined to sound as uninterested and cynical as possible. She knew her friends wouldn't let up if they knew she had even a particle of interest. And until she figured out how much interest there was on Dash's end, she wanted to avoid scrutiny.

"Come on, you like him, too, don't try to hide it," Alicia said, not giving up.

"He's not my type," Jamie said.

"And what is your type?" Alicia persisted.

"Let it go, and stop worrying about me," Jamie said. "My Latino prince will come."

Alicia and Carmen were intrigued. Did that mean Jamie would only date a Latino? She'd never implied that before.

"Dash's mother is Venezuelan. So he's half Latin," Alicia pointed out.

"Whatever." Jamie waved her hand as if she were

flicking away a fly. "He doesn't even play a real sport. Golf? What's wrong with football or basketball? Even tennis has more flava than golf."

Alicia groaned. "Here we go. It's the flava police again."

"Give it up," Carmen said. "You're an army of one with this whole flava thing. He's a cute guy."

"And clearly not a player like his friend, Troy," Alicia pointed out.

Carmen put on a deep voice, mimicking Troy: "One of you girls is going to leave your man for me."

Alicia followed suit: "Which one? Doesn't matter. My conquests are all interchangeable. Just like my corny lines."

"Hey, speaking of conquests, Domingo is working at Bongos tonight," Carmen said. "Do you guys want to come? Free virgin daiquiris all night long."

"We'll be there," Alicia said, as the boat pulled up to the dock. "Gaz and I love a freebie."

"Not tonight for me," Jamie said. "I've got a new collection of kicks that I'm working on. But I'll see you guys for lunch tomorrow."

Jamie started to walk away and then turned back around. "Oh, and, like, how do you say good-bye in Latina?"

"Shut up," Alicia said, laughing in spite of herself.

"Give the *pobrecita* a break," Carmen insisted.

"I think the one thing we can agree on is that Binky Mortimer is no poor little thing," Jamie said.

"*Pobrecita* doesn't mean 'poor little thing' in terms of the money you have in the bank," Carmen said. "It has to do with the sadness in your life, and while her mansion may be bangin', Binky lost her mother, and that sadness is real. So is her loneliness."

"True, dat," Alicia agreed.

"I guess so," Jamie said. But as she walked away, she still was not entirely sure she believed it.

After dinner that night, Jamie went out to her studio to work. The space was actually in the family garage. When they first moved in, Jamie's dad, Davide, had turned it into a shop for his woodworking. But as it turned out, since he was a limo driver who worked late most nights, he didn't actually have time to do much woodworking. As Jamie got more serious about her art, selling handmade items online and buying and selling vintage sneakers on eBay, she took over the garage space and turned it into a real artist's space. She painted the walls gallery white, and, instead of the single hanging bulb, filled the room with secondhand track lighting.

The studio was more than Jamie's work space. It was her hideaway. Whenever she was feeling stressed or confused about anything, she always felt better after she took out her spray paints and markers. She'd created a line of custom totes as party favors for Carmen's *quinceañera*, and the bags had been so popular that she was working on a new series, for her online shop on Etsy.com, a site where people could sell handmade jewelry, clothing, furniture, and all kinds of handcrafted items.

The new series was called Girls on Wheels, and the bags featured images of young women from all over the world on bicycles, motorbikes, and scooters. It was her favorite collection yet, and she hoped that it would sell out on Etsy. Just in time for the holidays.

Jamie loved the smell of paint on canvas. When she was a little girl, her mom, Zulema, had taken her to the museums in New York. Jamie would go up to all of the beautiful paintings and not only admire the images, but smell them. She wanted to smell the moon in Van Gogh's *The Starry Night* and the folds of Frida Kahlo's suit in *Self-Portrait with Cropped Hair*. It was a strange thing, she knew. But to her, it was like cooking. All of those layers of paints, all of those swirls of color, should smell like something—something good.

To satisfy her desire to experience art with her five senses—well, four senses, actually, since she didn't usually taste the art—her mother signed her up for an artist-in-residence program at El Museo del Barrio in New York City when Jamie was in the fifth grade. Every Saturday, she met with kids from all over the city and with her teacher, Trini Mayaguez. And one Saturday a month, they did studio visits and met with real artists in the apartments and studios where they worked.

It was at the Museo del Barrio where Jamie began to learn all the different techniques: portraiture; large-scale figure painting; and pictorial composition. But it was also that year when she learned that real paintings didn't have to have the quiet polished marble smell of a fancy museum. Paint fresh off an artist's brush smelled strong, bossy, bold, almost acidic, like lemonade without any sugar. Like Jamie herself.

"Knock-knock," Jamie's mother called through the garage door. "Up for company?"

"Sure," Jamie said, not surprised to see her. Her mom would often come in after dinner to visit. At the moment, Jamie was working on a character inspired by Alicia. But she was having a tough time getting the waves in Alicia's hair just right. It was a good time for a break anyway.

"I made hot chocolate," Jamie's mother said, handing her a cup.

Jamie was a miniature version of her mother, except that her mother's skin was a darker shade of mocha. Her stylishly close-cropped hair accentuated her high cheekbones. Where Jamie's style was hip-hop chic, Zulema favored clothes that had simple elegance, accessorized by her signature large silver hoop earrings.

"*Gracias, Mami.*"

Getting up from her work desk, Jamie took a seat on the old sofa that her mother had given her for the studio. The sofa had belonged to Jamie's grandmother, and as long as Jamie could remember before that, it had sat in her great-aunt's apartment in the Bronx, with a plastic slipcover on it. The first thing she'd done when the sofa arrived was to take the slipcover off. The mustard-colored upholstery was old and kind of ugly, but it still looked brand-new. Or, as her mother liked to say about hand-me-downs, "*Nuevo para ti.* New for you."

"So, tell me about your visit to the Mortimers. Do they really own an entire island, just for one family?" her mother asked. "You know, they devoted a whole episode to the Mortimers on *Miami Mansions, Townhouses and Villas.* I love those real-estate shows."

"Mom, it was crazy," Jamie said. "North pools, south

pools. East wings, west wings."

Her mother laughed. "And I bet it's not like a Latino family, where you've got half a dozen kids, the grandparents, aunts, uncles, cousins, all under one roof."

"Of course not. Just Binky, her brother, and their parents, and it's bigger than a college campus!" Jamie exclaimed. "It's like the place is designed so that every person in this tiny family has their own share of a giant kingdom. It's kind of disgusting."

"So, what inspired Binky to have a *quinceañera?*" her mother asked. "Doesn't seem to fit."

Jamie rolled her eyes.

"What?" her mother asked.

"It turns out that Binky's mother was Venezuelan," Jamie muttered.

Her mother grinned. "*Fíjate.* I love it. *The* Binky Mortimer is a secret Latina."

Jamie scowled. "She doesn't know anything about being Latina. She's a rich blond WASP who's dabbling in my culture."

"Whoa, *chica,*" her mother said. "Who died and made you head of the Latina police?"

"I'm just saying . . ."

"No, *niña,*" her mother interrupted. "Latinas come with all different backgrounds, skin tones, and hair colors. A lot of people look at me and think just because I have dark skin that I'm not Latina. You know the prejudice I've encountered from my own people. I will not stand for you holding Binky's money or her complexion against her."

Jamie stood and picked up her paintbrush. She didn't want to have a fight now. Not over Binky. Staring at the drawing in front of her, she thought about all the paintings she'd done of her mother's beautiful brown face. There must have been dozens. It made her sad that sometimes ignorant people treated her mother badly because they hadn't got the memo that the world was full of black Latinas. Maybe her mom had a point.

Perhaps sensing her daughter's discomfort, Zulema got up and walked over to the canvas. "I love your brush technique here," she said gently.

"Thanks," Jamie said.

Her mother looked as though she wanted to say something more, but she hesitated.

"Give Binky a chance," she urged finally. "Look at Alicia. Not every rich person is a carbon copy of the kids you knew when you went away to boarding school." She squeezed her daughter's shoulder.

"Whatever," Jamie muttered.

All of a sudden, she felt an inexplicable need to

clean all of her paintbrushes. She took them from the Bustelo coffee can that sat on the old wooden table next to her easel and walked over to the sink. She didn't want to talk about *it*. The past. She *never* talked about her past. She hoped her mother would get the hint and leave her alone.

No such luck.

"*Hija*, you know we were only trying to give you the best by sending you to that school."

Jamie was trying hard not to lose it, but it wasn't easy. If she had had a dollar for every time her parents had said they were trying to give her "the best" in referring to that stupid place, she wouldn't have had to sell sneakers on eBay for extra cash. And now, her mom was bringing up all that pain all over again.

As she continued carefully washing her paintbrushes with Johnson's Baby Shampoo, just as she'd learned to do in her Saturday morning art classes at El Museo del Barrio, she flashed back to sixth grade. They had still been living in the Bronx then. Everything had been a mess. A ten-year-old kid had pulled a gun on a teacher when she asked him for his homework. The gun wasn't loaded, but the incident had been front-page news all over the country. Metal detectors were installed at the school. Officers patrolled the outside of the school as well as the lunchroom.

Jamie's parents had freaked, even though she'd kept insisting she wasn't scared. Still, Jamie's social-worker-in-training mother had a zero-tolerance policy when it came to kids in bad situations. If a kid was in danger, her first priority was getting them out. And that went double for her own daughter. Without even talking to Jamie about it, Zulema had pulled some strings and gotten Jamie a scholarship at Fitzgibbons Academy, a snooty boarding school in Connecticut. And when Jamie protested, Zulema and Davide had made it clear that it wasn't up for discussion. They were ordering her to go, and one day, she would thank them. It was what was "best for her."

So off to boarding school in Connecticut Jamie Sosa went, and what followed was the most emotionally challenging experience she had had in her young life.

Six months later, Jamie's father's dad had died suddenly of a heart attack. Her parents decided to move to Miami to help take care of his wife, Cristina, and so that her father could run the family car-service business. Jamie had been terrified that she was going to have to stay at Fitzgibbons. But, as Zulema had explained, there wasn't enough money to fly her back and forth between Connecticut and Miami for holiday visits. She'd have had to be up there on her own, and that was not something Zulema could live with. She wanted her daughter close.

Jamie didn't argue. Six months had been plenty, in her opinion. She'd been a fish out of water, the target of cruel jokes from overprivileged rich girls who had no intention of welcoming a brown-skinned scholarship student from the Bronx into the fold. They had gone out of their way to ostracize her, giving her mean nicknames, kicking her out of the cafeteria, even, at one point, destroying a painting she'd been working on—something she'd been planning to show at the Parents' Weekend Art Show.

And then there were the guys—confident, slick, and used to getting whatever they wanted. It seemed that many of them made the assumption that just because she was receiving financial aid and was the school's only Latina student, she would do anything to fit in. Jamie, who had never even dated but had always been part of the popular crowd in her own school, now found herself in way over her head. She had retreated into herself, hiding away and losing the sense of independence on which she had prided herself in New York.

She hadn't hated *every* second of it. After all, it was her art teacher, Masako Utada, who'd turned her on to the hand-painted sneaker scene on eBay, fueled in large part by a huge demand in Japan. She probably never would've learned about that in the South Bronx.

But that was one good thing in a sea of bad.

She'd jumped at the chance to ditch boarding school and the daily chore of being a cultural anthropologist among the young, wealthy, and cruel.

Moving to Miami meant more than a chance to live back at home with her parents, whom she was loath to admit she had missed while she'd been away at school. The move to Coral Gables was a chance for her to reinvent herself. She was no longer Jamie Sosa, shy and slightly awkward scholarship kid at the Big Fancy Boarding School. She was Jamie Sosa, cooler-than-you babe from the Bronx.

But, while it had worked and Jamie loved her new life, moments like this—heart-to-heart talks with her mother and run-ins with people like Binky, who so clearly reminded her of the past—were still harder to get through than she liked to admit. She could only hope that taking on this *quinceañera* wasn't going to send her running for the shadows again.

CHAPTER 5

THE NEXT afternoon, Binky arrived at Alicia's house ready to hammer out the details of her *quince*. Everyone was there except Gaz, who was once again working.

"So, as we mentioned yesterday, the most important thing we need to do is come up with a theme for your *quince*," Alicia explained when they had all made themselves comfortable in the Florida room.

"Exactly," Carmen agreed. "As we said, the theme will dictate everything, from the decorations to your dress—which I needed to design and start making *yesterday*."

"Well, then, let's get started, because my motto is 'go big or go home'!" Binky said. "After y'all left, I thought a lot about it. Did you know I'm a junior member of the Daughters of the American Revolution?"

She was met with blank looks.

"Forgive my ignorance," Alicia said, stifling a giggle, "but what are the Daughters of the American Revolution? Is it a voter's drive, like MTV's Choose or Lose?"

"Oh, no, nothing like that. It's so cool," Binky said.

"I doubt it," Jamie muttered.

If Binky heard Jamie's snarky aside, she didn't let it show. Beaming, she explained, "The Daughters of the American Revolution is a volunteer organization made up of women who are descended from the first families in America."

"You mean the Native Americans?" Jamie asked, feigning sweetness.

"No, I mean the first families who came over from Britain," Binky said, struggling to remain cheerful, even though Jamie's mockery was getting to her.

"Right, the ones who brought over the epidemics that wiped out entire tribes; got it," Jamie said, standing up and heading for the kitchen.

"Let her finish!" Alicia said.

"Finish, finish!" Jamie said as she walked out of the room. "I find Binky's ancestors' role in the annihilation of an entire people nothing short of fascinating."

When she was out of the earshot, Binky looked at Carmen and Alicia, a confused expression on her face. "Why does she hate me so much?" she asked.

"She doesn't hate you," Carmen said.

"Wealth makes her uncomfortable," Alicia explained. "Believe me, I know from experience. But once you're down with her, you will not find a more loyal friend than Jamie."

Jamie reentered the Florida room with a tray of empanadas and some bottles of Jarritos. "Maribelle, the Cruz family cook, sent these," she told Binky. "Please continue. I won't interrupt."

Binky took a deep breath. "As I was saying, I was thinking about going with a colonial theme. I could wear a powdered wig and a gown with satin and ruffles, and then I could descend from a full-scale replica of the *Mayflower*."

Alicia and Carmen made concerted efforts not to crack up.

"It's certainly a unique idea," Carmen said.

"But there are, um, some logistical challenges," Alicia added diplomatically.

Binky looked at Jamie. "Don't tell me you don't have an opinion?"

Jamie shrugged. "If you don't have anything nice to say . . ."

"Come on," Binky pleaded. "I hired you guys to plan my *quinceañera* because everyone says you're the best.

I want my *quince* to rock. So if you think the idea sucks, just tell me."

"Okay, I don't love it," Alicia said.

"It's a little old-fashioned," Carmen added.

"It sucks," Jamie said, flat out.

"That's better. Thank you for your honesty." Binky smiled. "So, if my colonial history isn't going to cut it, what *do* you think I should do?"

"Well," Jamie said. "You live on that incredible island. You could have a Bali-themed island-paradise *quince*. Maybe we could turn your cabanas into gilded temples, and your dress could be inspired by an Indonesian goddess."

Binky clapped her hands and, for a moment, looked like a little girl in a candy shop. "I love it!"

Alicia pantomimed tipping her hat at Jamie. "Nice one, my friend."

Carmen looked thoughtful. "I don't know," she said slowly. "The whole Indonesian goddess thing seems over the top. We want to focus on Binky's Latina heritage, not just the fact that she's got beaucoup bucks. After all, that is what you said, right, Binky? That you want to get in touch with your roots?"

Binky nodded. "I do. My mother's family came from a small island off the mainland of Venezuela. I'd love somehow to give a nod to her."

"So, what about 'Princess of the Tides'?" Carmen suggested. "It brings the island theme in, with the idea of a journey across water to arrive at your destination."

Binky nodded again. "I *do* want this to be meaningful. Princess of the Tides is *perfect*."

Jamie didn't look displeased by the idea. "You've got those boats; work that, too. Pick everyone up at Biscayne Bay in your yacht, ride 'em around for an hour, then have the actual party back at your pool."

"But what about the church ceremony?" Carmen asked. "I'm sure Binky's mom wouldn't have wanted her to just throw a big party to celebrate her heritage. The spiritual element is part of what makes a *quince* something special. It's not just a Latina version of *My Super Sweet 16*."

Binky smiled. "Love that show, but you're right. I want to get all the traditional *quince* stuff in, too, in honor of my mom and because that's how Estrella said I should do it. It's my coming into womanhood, so I want to do it right. Could I have people meet me at the church, then be bused to the yacht, then ferried over to the island?"

"That's a lot of juggling. Means a lot of cooperation from everyone. How does the rest of your family feel about your having a *quince*?" Jamie asked. "I'm sure it's not anything the Mortimer family has seen before."

Binky smiled. "Well, actually, everyone's getting into it. Dash has been to a few *quinces*, and I think he's a little jealous that there wasn't a guy-equivalent so he could bust out his flawless Spanish and impress everybody. Bev, my stepmother, is excited, but she wanted me to have the events coordinator at the country club organize it. She doesn't care what I call my fifteenth birthday as long as it's swank enough to impress her friends. And my dad, he doesn't say much about anything. He's a little bit of the strong-and-silent type."

Just then, Gaz entered the room, fresh from his shift at the Gap. His dark, curly hair, beautiful brown eyes, and lips that seemed always to be on the verge of forming a slightly wicked smile all brightened the room. "Did somebody call for the strong-and-silent type?"

Alicia got up and gave him a kiss. "So conceited! We weren't talking about you. I was beginning to wonder if you'd skipped town on me."

"Never," Gaz said. "You know the deal, I'm just the hardest-working guy in Coral Gables right now. Tough to do that and be a good boyfriend, too."

"You're always a good boyfriend," Alicia said,

squeezing his hand. She turned to Binky. "Binky Mortimer, this is my boyfriend, Gaz. He's also a member of Amigas Inc. and in charge of music for the *quinceañera*. You'll be talking to him a lot as we get closer to the event."

"Nice to meet you," Binky said politely.

"Mucho gusto," Gaz said, shaking Binky's hand. Then he nodded at Jamie and Carmen. "What up, *chicas*? Is there anything to eat in the kitchen? I'm starving."

"Of course. Help yourself, but hurry back; we need you," Alicia said.

The girls were silent for a moment, staring down at the clipboards in their hands. These had been presents and were engraved with the words AMIGAS INC. They came in handy at moments like this, when the girls needed to jot ideas down. Having the company name on the clipboards made them all feel extra professional.

"I don't know," Alicia said, breaking the silence and getting back to the topic at hand. "I just think that if you start at the church, then have people take a bus to the boat and then a boat to the island, it feels a little like too much is going on."

"Yeah," Binky said, nodding her head in agreement. "I don't want people so exhausted by the time they get to the island that they're too pooped to party."

"What if the entire party took place on the yacht?" Jamie suggested. "People get married at sea; couldn't we do Binky's ceremony *on* the boat?"

"We'd have to talk to her priest," Carmen said.

Binky fluttered her eyelids dramatically. "You mean, my very good-looking, very young priest. That shouldn't be a problem."

"You're kidding, right?" Alicia asked.

"*Not* kidding. He looks like Chace Crawford," Binky said. "I have proof. His name is Padre Alfonso. Some of the parishioners have even built a little fan site about him." Taking out her smartphone, Binky pulled up the site. She passed the phone around. "Ladies, meet Padre Alfonso."

The girls crowded around, mesmerized by the photos of the *Gossip Girl*–worthy priest, including one somewhat unpriestly photo of him in a pair of yellow swimming trunks.

"What's up with the swimsuit calendar shot?" Jamie asked.

"Catholic church retreat," Binky said. "Isn't he dreamy?"

"You know, I really think I need to talk to my parents about switching churches," Alicia said.

"Not me." Carmen shook her head. "Can you

imagine going to confession with a guy who was so good-looking? It's a tiny little box; I'd be so nervous I'd probably develop a stuttering problem."

"I'd be too tempted to lie," Jamie said. "I couldn't confess anything about making out with boys to a guy who looked like that."

Binky raised an eyebrow. "At our church, we have exactly that problem. So many women were going into confession with wild stories that couldn't possibly be true that they had to take Padre Alfonso off confession duty!"

"Unbelievable," Alicia said, her eyes wide.

"That's bananas," Carmen laughed.

"Maybe giving your church such an eye-candyish priest is God's way of saying, 'Get your butt here every Sunday,'" Jamie said, smiling.

Binky placed her hand over her heart. "Well, I haven't missed a Sunday this year, so it must be working!"

Just then, Alicia looked at her watch and let out a little gasp. "While I personally could talk about the sin-inspiring hottie priest all day, we've got exactly four weeks and five days to pull off the *quinceañera* of the year. We've got to focus. We have a theme. And I'll go ahead and make an appointment with Padre Hottie—I mean, Padre Alfonso—to see if he would be willing to do Binky's *quince* ceremony on the yacht." She wrote something on her clipboard.

"Way to take one for the team," Jamie said, winking at her friend.

Gaz came back to the room and stood in the door. "Are you still talking about your crush on the priest? Because I'd really like to join the meeting."

"We're done," Jamie said, waving him in. "Join us."

She quickly filled Gaz in on the Princess of Tides theme.

"We've never done a *quince* on a boat," Gaz said. "That sounds pretty sweet. Do you know yet whether you want a DJ or live music?"

"We recommend live," Alicia chimed in.

"Live music, definitely," Binky agreed.

Gaz handed her a CD. "This is my band's music. Listen and see what you think. If it's totally not your thing, we can hire another group or look into the DJ option. It's your big day, so we want to do what will make you happy."

"Trust me, Binky. Gaz's band is straight off the hook. He's one of the hottest up-and-coming indie musicians in the Miami area. You and your friends are going to go nuts when you hear his music. He's that good," boasted Alicia.

Gaz rolled his eyes as Binky laughed good-naturedly. "And, of course, you're not prejudiced or anything, right?"

"Me? Never," replied Alicia, feigning shock at the thought. "Okay, moving on. Logistics," she continued. They had the venue—hopefully—and the priest—double-hopefully—but that was just the start. "How many people can you fit on the *Santa Maria*?"

"Oh, we wouldn't have it on the *Santa Maria*. She's not a yacht, she's just the ferryboat," Binky said. "The big boat is the *Uptick*. My dad had a company retreat on it last year, and I think they said that the capacity was two hundred fifty. That's plenty; I wasn't planning on inviting more than that."

"Great," Alicia said. "Well, you talk to your father about the *quince* and make sure he signs off on using the boat, and let's find out out what kind of restrictions they might have about safety, medical care, catering, and having minors on board."

Binky looked surprised. "Whoa, way to sound so grown-up."

Alicia shrugged. "It's our business, and we've learned a lot along the way."

"Well, I'm impressed," Binky said.

Alicia smiled and once again looked down at her

clipboard. "Okay. Invitations. We need to get them out right away. Jamie, can you handle that?"

Jamie wrote something down on her own clipboard. "Of course. Binky, any requests?"

"Hmm . . . Well, as I told you, orange is my signature color," she said. "So, something with that?"

"Right, I remember you said that." Jamie skimmed the *quince* planning guidelines that Alicia had typed up for Amigas Inc.

"Orange is a good base. What are you thinking Jamie?" Alicia asked. "I bet you have some ideas already."

Jamie turned to a clean sheet of her notepad and drew a sketch. "I was thinking with the theme that it would be so cool if the invitations came as a message in a bottle, with seashells and filled with sand."

"What do you think, Binky?" Alicia asked.

"I love it," she said. "Maybe I could handwrite each invite with a special message to my guests."

"Well, that would depend what your handwriting is like," Carmen said. She'd been quiet for a while, sketching on her own pad.

Binky made a face. "My handwriting bites."

"I can do them," said Jamie. "I did that course in calligraphy."

"Awesome," Alicia said. "This is going great. What's next?"

"If the invitation is in a bottle, then we're going to need to deliver each one personally," Jamie said. "You can't put these in the mail."

"Sounds like a job for the boyfriends," Carmen said, smiling slyly.

Gaz took the opportunity to interject, "Because message-in-a-bottle invitations are *so-o-o* manly." He shot a look at Alicia but then smiled. "We'll do it. I'll get Domingo to help."

"Who's Domingo?" Binky asked.

"He's my boyfriend. He goes to Hialeah High and works part-time at Bongos," Carmen said.

"And what about you?" Binky asked, turning and eyeing Jamie.

"What *about* me?"

Alicia and Carmen tried to send Binky a mental message to stop before she got in over her head, but their attempts at telepathy failed.

"You've got it going on," Binky told Jamie. "You must have a boyfriend."

Surprisingly, Jamie had calmed down since Binky first arrived. In fact, she had been feeling mellow. Although she was loath to admit it, and probably never would unless forced to in a court of law, Jamie could see that Binky was kind of a fun girl to hang out with. But her questions about guys were rubbing Jamie the wrong way, and she quickly fell into her defensive mode.

"Nope. I haven't met a guy who's a good enough salsa dancer to roll with me," she stated.

"Ple-e-e-e-ase let me set you up with my brother." Binky held her hands up in mock prayer. "He likes you, I can tell. And he's amazing on the dance floor."

Jamie laughed. "Mr. Sponge Golf Square Pants dancing salsa? Come on, now."

But Binky shook her head. "Believe it. My father always said, 'Never underestimate a Mortimer.'" Suddenly she got a look on her face as if a lightbulb had gone off. "What are you all doing tomorrow night?"

"Planning your *quince*," Alicia said.

"Researching looks for your *quince* dress," said Carmen.

"Handwriting two hundred and fifty *quince* invitations and placing each one of them in a bottle," Jamie finished, her tone a bit sharp.

But this didn't faze Binky in the slightest. "All of those things are, I agree, of vital importance, since I want my *quinceañera* to be the best one that South Florida has ever seen. But I think there is something else you need to do. You *need* to come dancing with me tomorrow night. Alicia—you can show me some ideas for choreography. Plus, Jamie can see what an amazing dancer Dash is."

"We've still got to work on the guest list and the seating arrangements. Then we have to decide on your centerpieces," Alicia said, a little unconvincingly.

"You could do that at the club!" Binky said.

"Gaz usually plays the father-daughter *vals*, but you'll need to decide whether you want his band to play all night or whether you want to hire a DJ for the after-party," Carmen added.

"We could do *that* at the club!"

"And I would love to show you sketches for your dress."

"Club; club; club!" Binky chanted.

"Okay, fine; we'll go. Need to make the customer happy," Alicia said, relenting when it was obvious Binky wasn't going to give up.

"I suppose I'm down," Carmen said.

"Sounds like a plan," Gaz added.

"I guess I'm in, too," Jamie said.

Binky squealed excitedly. "This is going to be so fun! I've got to go home and pick out an outfit. And call Dash." She leaped up and then turned to Jamie. "He's going to be so happy to hear you're coming."

Blowing air kisses to the group, Binky ran out of the room, her fingers already on the speed-dial button of her phone.

"Whatever," Jamie said to the girl's retreating back, pretending not to care.

But, as Amigas Inc. continued to divvy up responsibilities for planning Binky's *quince*, Jamie felt the kind of giggly anticipation about seeing a cute boy that she hadn't felt in a long, *long* time.

CHAPTER 6

EVER SINCE Ojos Así opened, it had been the hottest nightclub for the under-21 crowd in Biscayne Bay. This meant that, despite the fact that Alicia, Carmen, Jamie, and even Gaz were dressed to the nines in their favorite outfits, they were still having trouble getting inside.

"Join the line, my friends," said a tall guy who looked not unlike an FBI agent in his dark gray pinstriped suit. It was only the fact that he wore sunglasses at night that gave away his role as one of Miami's glitterati enforcers.

"This sucks," Alicia said, walking away from the crowd with her friends.

"Where are Binky and Dash?" Carmen asked, looking around.

"Maybe we should go somewhere else," suggested Gaz.

"Or maybe we should just all go home," Jamie said.

"Who wants to spend good money to watch a bunch of rich prep-school kids turn a fierce merengue into a chicken dance."

"Let's not give up yet," Alicia said. "This could be a lot of fun. And not *everyone* in there is going to be preppy and ruining your vision of Latino life. Let's try this again."

The members of Amigas Inc.—most especially Alicia—were not used to being turned away at any velvet rope. They weren't part of the hard-core party crowd at C. G. High, but, as increasingly successful *quinceañera* planners, they were starting to get to know the players on Miami's nightclub scene. And Gaz accepted the fact that Alicia sometimes resorted to doing a little pretend flirting if it helped get them all in the door.

As she was about to do right now.

"Excuse me," she said, returning to stand in front of the doorman, tossing her hair to the side. "I don't think I caught your name."

"Dwight," he said.

"Dwight," Alicia said, smiling. "Didn't you used to work at Flip?"

"No, I didn't." Dwight said. He turned back to the crowd. "Anybody here actually on the guest list? No? Then I have four words for you: *Back of the line.*"

He turned to Alicia, Carmen, Jamie, and Gaz. "That means you, too."

The crew retreated to the back of the line.

"I hate these waiting games," Jamie said.

"What can you do? Sometimes the magic works, sometimes it just doesn't." Alicia shivered a little bit and snuggled up close to Gaz. Her Missoni knit dress was not nearly as warm as it looked. Despite the hot days in Miami, the evenings could get quite chilly.

"How could he turn away so much fabulous?" Jamie said. "I mean, look at me. Vintage Ossie Clark dress from Resurrection in L.A. limited-edition four-inch leather booties from Jimmy Choo for H&M. Lucite bangles from Lanvin, also vintage. I've got more style in my little finger than any of these spandex-wearing Miami girls have in their entire bodies. They'd be lucky to have me in their stupid club."

Just then, a voice from behind them said, "I couldn't agree more."

Startled, Jamie whirled around, nearly toppling over. She found herself alarmingly close to Dash, who had an amused grin on his handsome face. Binky stood next to him, looking amazing in a Herve Leger dress that, while clearly made of much nicer fabric, was still tight and still short.

"Eavesdrop much?" Jamie asked, standing nose to nose with Dash.

"Boast about yourself much?" Dash countered.

"No more than you, I'm sure," Jamie said.

Binky yanked her brother's arm playfully. "Would you two stop flirting? Dash, come meet Gaz. He's the musical genius behind Amigas Incorporated."

The two guys shook hands and exchanged the usual "Good to meet you, man" greetings.

"Now," said Binky, "move your butt and get us in the club."

Dash nodded good-naturedly. Turning to Jamie, he boasted, "Watch how a master does it."

They followed him to the front of the line, but before Dash even spoke, Dwight reached out his hand. "My man. Nice to see you. Still making that green on the green?"

"I am," Dash said, shaking Dwight's hand.

"Well, it's nice to see you," the bouncer said. "Who's in your party?"

Dash pointed to the Amigas and Binky. "Meet my friends Alicia, Carmen, and Gaz. You know my sister, Binky, and this is my new friend, Jamie." The way he said, "friend," made it seem as though he were hoping to make it more.

"Right this way," the bouncer said, lifting the velvet rope so the group could sail through. "You all have a good time."

"Oh, we will, *Dwight*," Alicia said, giving him a little wave. Then she whispered to Gaz and Carmen, "We're in." And Carmen whispered to Jamie, "We're in." And Jamie said out loud, "Another pretentious nightclub; who cares?"

Jamie was soon forced to take back her words. The club was hardly what they were expecting. Unlike most of the Miami hotspots, Ojos Así was totally futuristic, with Japanese-inspired decor. The stark white walls were illuminated by purple and green lights that flashed across them like spaceships in a video game. A giant sushi conveyor belt came down from the ceiling and wound around the lounge area. Several Dance Dance Revolution stations were lined up along the back wall.

"Who's hungry?" Binky asked. Immediately, Carmen raised both of her hands.

"Great," said Binky. "Anyone else? Sashimi or hand roll?"

"Tasty," Alicia said.

"You know I'm in," Gaz said, following Binky, Carmen, and Alicia to the conveyor-belt counter.

That left Dash and Jamie—alone. At first, she tried

to look everywhere but at him. She looked at the dance floor, at the main floor, at the door to the bathroom, but the whole time, she could feel his gaze on her and she shivered, involuntarily. Distance had apparently made her heart grow fonder. Or maybe she was just seeing reality for the first time. What had she been thinking? He wasn't just "okay," as she'd told herself while lying in bed. He was freaking handsome. Dirty-blond hair, ever so slightly in need of a haircut. Check. Chiseled cheekbones. Check. Perfectly kissable cupid's-bow lips, electric blue eyes. Check, check. It wasn't even that he was particularly Jamie's type. It was more that he was the type for any woman with a pulse and clear vision—which apparently she now had. He was textbook handsome in a way that could have been kind of boring, but he was just scruffy enough that he was irresistible.

"You hungry, too?" he asked, interrupting her mental size-up. "Or interested in something with more substance—like getting to know me?"

For Jamie, it was like a particularly wicked round of Truth or Dare. Was she going to tell the truth to herself, and to Dash, and admit that she was interested in learning more about him? Interested in seeing if there were more to him than good looks? Or would she turn and follow her friends to the swirl of California rolls and unagi making its way down the conveyor belt and walk away from what could possibly be the coolest guy she'd met since she'd moved to Miami?

She took a deep breath and called out to Alicia, Carmen, and Binky, "I'll catch up with you guys later."

Smiling, Dash took her hand and led her to a little table tucked into a quiet corner. He signaled a waiter and ordered them both Kyoto spritzers.

"I know this club is a little bit Miami flash," he said when they had made themselves comfortable. "But I've been a fan of DJ Lucia since I was in junior high. I used to download her mixes off of MySpace. She blends old-school Latin music with everything from the Beatles to Beck."

Jamie raised an eyebrow. "You're really into music for a golf nerd," she teased.

"I think the term you're looking for is 'golf *champ*,'" Dash said, correcting her.

Jamie tried to conceal the fact that she was impressed. "What tournaments have you won, exactly?"

"Three time Junior World champ, but I don't like to brag—or jinx myself. So, since I want to avoid that, let's talk about you. Tell me everything about you, Jamie Sosa," Dash said, his smile a picket fence of perfectly white teeth.

Jamie could feel her face flush. Even though she didn't know him, she had a strange urge to do as he said and open up. Tell him things she hadn't even told Alicia and Carmen.

And she suddenly wondered if that was what poets and philosophers meant by "love at first sight." Not merely the desire to kiss a guy the moment you met him and kiss him again and again for the rest of your life (that, she had to admit, she felt), but the desire to tell a guy everything—as if the "friend" part of "boyfriend" were lit up in neon lights. Because, when Dash had said, "Tell me everything about you," she hadn't had the urge to feed him the same old practiced lines about growing up in the boogie-down, about how being from the birthplace of salsa and hip-hop had inspired her fashion and her art—even though those things were very much true.

Jamie Sosa wanted to tell Dash that even though she was always talking about how great the Bronx was, part of the time she had lived there it had really been a struggle. She wanted to tell him about how her father had worked two jobs six days a week, going from his day job as a shipping clerk to his night-watchman job in the evenings, and how her mother had used to work in a factory and had had to leave the house at four a.m.

to take two trains and a bus to get to work. She wanted to tell him about how one day she'd been walking home from school and she looked across the street and all the kids started dropping to the ground, and she turned around, and right behind her there was this guy with a gun, jumping out of a car, pointing and shooting. She'd never heard a gun fired before then. She was ten years old, and all she could think was how the shots really went "bang, bang," just the way they wrote in books.

She wanted to tell Dash that although nobody on her block had been shot that day, the incident scared her mother so much that she wasn't allowed to play outside anymore. She had to go to school, come straight home, and call her mother the minute she got inside.

And inside wasn't much better than outside. The walls of their rental apartment were a stark white, and when she asked her parents why they didn't have any pictures in frames like at school, her father had said, "We don't have money for that, *niña*." So, one day, when the blankness finally got to be too much, Jamie borrowed some art supplies from school and began painting on the walls.

When her mother came home from work that night and saw the painted walls, she woke Jamie up and threatened to ground her for the rest of her life.

"This isn't our apartment, *chica*," her mother said. "If the landlord sees this, he'll throw us out on our ear." But the next morning, she decided that she liked what she saw, and she told Jamie to keep painting and leave the landlord to her. Seeing how happy it made their daughter, her parents started taking her to museums on Sundays. They took her to places like the Museum of Modern Art, the Met, the Brooklyn Museum, the Museum of Natural History. They went to them all.

Jamie wanted to tell Dash how lonely and miserable she had felt at boarding school, how out of place she had been, how cruel people could be. Or how it had taken nearly three years from the time the guy had shot at people outside of their building for her mother to finish her master's degree in social work and get a job working in social services. And longer still for their family to move out of Jamie's grandmother's cramped cottage into the little house her uncle had found for them in Coral Gables. Or how, although Jamie hadn't wanted to stay in the Bronx, when the time had come, she had been scared to leave it. And the last thing that Jamie and her parents had done before they left for the airport was to paint each wall of their dingy little apartment white again. "That is my story," she would tell him.

But this was only her first date with Dash—and it was only sort of a date, at that. It was technically a *quince*-related get-together with Binky. And she couldn't spill her guts in a noisy nightclub to a preppy rich boy whom she'd only just met, love or no love. So instead, she took a sip of her drink and said, "The DJ is playing my song. Let's dance."

Truth be told, she considered anything by Pitbull her song. And she needed a break from her thoughts. She ran onto the dance floor. Seconds later, Dash was beside her, matching her step for step—no small move when the music was booming at 120 beats per minute.

"You're good," Dash whispered in her ear, as his hands slipped around her waist and he pulled her close.

"You should see me when I'm bad," she said, winking at him. "I'm much, much better." She didn't know what it was about this boy—they hadn't spent any real time together, but she felt much more comfortable with him than she had with any of the guys she went to school with—which was bananas, because the guys at C. G. High were public school guys, and Dash was so much the textbook opposite that he might as well have had tattooed over each eyebrow the words *preppy* and *rich*. In any case, here she was, flirting and dancing with a prepster. She felt a stirring of something new, something real. As if maybe it weren't all about being one thing *or* the other.

When the others joined them for a few songs, Jamie's mood stayed high. Binky's dancing was as hopeless as her Spanish, but there was a certain charm to her total lack of rhythm that carried her through.

Jamie would have been happy if the night never ended. But at ten forty-five, Alicia looked at her watch and sighed. "I'm about to turn into a pumpkin. My dad will be here in fifteen minutes to pick Gaz and me up. Who else needs a ride?"

"I'm exhausted," Carmen said.

"Me, too," Binky agreed. "What about you, Jamie?"

Jamie looked at Dash quickly, out of the corner of her eye. She wanted to stay, but she didn't want to assume he'd take her home.

"I'll make sure Jamie gets back safely," Dash said, as if reading her mind. He turned to her. "If that's okay with you."

She nodded. It felt as if her head were no longer connected to her neck. As if reality had gone out the window.

Binky smiled knowingly. Then she gave her brother a big hug and reached for Jamie's hand. But Jamie was too quick to get caught in a hug. Looking down at her dress, she said, "I'm too sweaty," and gave Binky a double-cheek kiss instead.

An hour after everyone had left, Jamie and Dash were still enjoying each other's company. She'd taken off her high heels and was enthusiastically dancing barefoot. The DJ shifted into *cumbia*, and Dash took her in his arms and began to swing her around with the finesse of an old Dominican *abuelo* who had been a professional dancer back in the day.

Jamie had never been the biggest fan of traditional music, because she really abhorred the notion prevalent in Latin dance that the man had to lead and the woman had to follow. She loved dancing with her father, and when she was a kid, she had loved dancing with her grandfather before he passed away. But letting some pimply teenage boy—a guy her own age—"lead" . . . Well, forgive the cliché, but no way, José.

Still, as with everything else, dancing with Dash was . . . different. It wasn't so much that he was leading, though he was obviously the better dancer. But what it suddenly felt like to Jamie, what she now understood for maybe the first time as he spun and dipped her and glided her from one side of the dance floor to the other, was that dancing was a conversation. And the things she couldn't—wouldn't—tell him yet in words, she could say with her moves.

In honors English that year, their class had read James Joyce's *Ulysses*. Jamie, who had found it interminable, had pretty much skimmed it, despite her teacher's assertion that assigning them Joyce had been like giving them Christmas and Easter and the Fourth of July all rolled into one.

Now, dancing with Dash, feeling the back and forth of his steps, all she could think of was the last line of Joyce's book, from Molly Bloom's soliloquy. The prose told about a girl who wasn't sure how to let herself fall in love. A girl who finally decided to take a leap and just say yes. Just as Jamie was deciding now. Yes, Jamie kept thinking, yes, I said yes, I will, yes.

CHAPTER 7

IT WAS NEARLY two a.m. when Dash pulled up in front of the Sosa house. Jamie sat in his mini Cooper convertible and tried to keep the silly grin off her face.

"Well, I had a nice time," Dash said after a moment of silence.

Understatement of the year, Jamie thought, catching a glimpse of herself in the car's side mirror. Her face was still sweaty—Carmen would have said, "dewy," but Jamie called it what it was: sweaty. Dash, on the other hand, looked as if he'd just come from a leisurely day at the beach.

"I had a nice time, too," Jamie said, looking out the window, and praying that her mother had gotten her text message that she was out late, but hadn't sat up waiting.

Dash looked at her, as if contemplating what he would say next. For a moment, Jamie wondered if the amazing night had all been in her imagination. And then he asked, "Would it be okay if I kissed you?"

Jamie sighed, stalling as she remembered the first time she had kissed a boy. Her mind flashed back to the Bronx. It had been so embarrassing. Fifth grade. Spin the bottle. Reinaldo Lopez. The moment had left a lot to be desired. Now she tried to think of something smart-alecky and clever to reply. But she couldn't. So she just said the word that had been in her mind all night: "Yes."

Then his lips were on hers. They were pillow-soft, and Jamie felt herself get lost in the moment. This was unlike any kiss she'd had before—not that there had been many of those.

Dash was an excellent kisser. So much so that Jamie soon found that trying to kiss him just once was like opening a bag of M&M's and trying to eat just one. She kissed him again and again, happy, surprised that she'd found this person who could make her feel so comfort-able and so good.

Then she heard it. She felt it. Dash had unsnapped her bra.

She pulled away. "What do you think you're doing?" she asked.

"I'm sorry." Dash held up his hands. "It was an accident."

"Bras are actually intricate pieces of technology," Jamie said, growing furious. "They don't come off by accident."

"I mean, it was an accident because I wasn't thinking when I did it," Dash said. Jamie couldn't tell from the aggrieved expression on his face if he were genuinely sorry or just annoyed that she had pulled back.

"Clearly you weren't," Jamie said, her voice barely containing the rage she now felt. How could everything have been so perfect five seconds ago? She felt as if she'd been thrown back into boarding school. "Just because I don't have money like you, just because I'm from the Bronx, you think you can slide to second just like that? I bet you wouldn't try that with one of the girls from your fancy prep school."

Reaching for the handle, she flung the car door open and jumped out. She slammed it behind her, not caring if it woke up the neighborhood.

Dash jumped out after her. "It was stupid. You're just so beautiful, and I was so in the moment. . . ."

"Well, guess what?" Jamie hissed. "That moment is gone, and you'll never see the likes of it again." Turning, she walked up the path to her house, leaving a flustered Dash behind her.

Jamie opened the front door as quietly as she could.

It was completely dark except for the light over the kitchen table. On it was a note from her mother:

Late night, hija. Don't make it a habit. Wake me when you get in, so I know you're okay.

Jamie went in and said good night to her parents and then went to her room and changed into her pajamas. She brushed her teeth and, as she always did, ever since she was a little girl, double-checked the locks on the front door. Through the peephole, she could see that Dash was still sitting in his car out front. It was a futile exercise. A cow would jump over the moon before she gave him a second chance.

But as she climbed into her bed, she couldn't help wondering, if Dash was the one who had messed up, why did it feel as though, in walking away, she was not hurting him but punishing herself? Why was *she* the one crying herself to sleep in bed?

The next morning, Jamie woke up to the sound of her phone alarm playing an old Pitbull tune. The pulsating beat brought all of the memories of the evening before back. Groaning, she turned it off and stuck her head under her pillow.

She'd had *such* a good time with Dash. Too bad it had turned out that she'd had him figured out correctly the first time. He was an entitled, golf-club-swinging prepster. And he'd thought he could get into her pants just because she was from the hood.

She let out a big sigh. There was no time for dwelling on it. She was supposed to meet Binky and the girls in—she looked at her phone—twenty minutes ago! She jumped out of bed, brushed her teeth, took the world's quickest shower, and begged her mother for a ride.

Walking into Bongos, she began apologizing as soon as she saw her girls. "*Discúlpenme, chicas.* I kept hitting snooze, and, well, you know the way that movie ends."

There was a seat open next to Binky, but Jamie squeezed into the booth with Carmen instead.

"My future sister-in-law!" Binky squealed, getting up to give Jamie a giant hug. "I told Alicia and Carmen that you were bound to be late. Dash didn't get home until almost five."

"And since we know the club closed at one . . ." Carmen began.

"We couldn't help but wonder what you were doing for four hours!" Alicia gave Jamie a probing glance. "Is there something that you want to tell us?"

There was a part of Jamie that really wanted to talk to her friends about the evening, tell them how confusing it had been, and get their help in figuring out why spending time with Dash had reminded her of great novels. Last night, she had felt like Molly Bloom in *Ulysses*. This morning, after all that fun dancing followed by Dash's totally lecherous pass at her, the phrase that came to mind was from Dickens: the best of times and the worst of times. But she couldn't say anything. It was her own fault. She had let vulnerable Jamie out to play, and that Jamie had ended up with a heart that, while not broken, was definitely bruised. She was going to have to go back to being Jamie from the block. Much safer that way. And much safer not to let the girls in on something that would amount to nothing in the future anyway.

Luckily, she was saved from further discussion when Domingo approached them, dressed in his waiter uniform of crisp white shirt, black tie, and black pants. It was here at Bongos, unofficial Amigas headquarters, that Carmen and Domingo had met. He was already thick as thieves with the rest of the group, helping them to create a Web site and advising them on all things technical.

"*Hola,* gorgeous," he said, winking at Carmen. "*Hola, amigas.* I would ask for your order, but I think I know—crab empanadas, *plátanos,* black beans, and rice."

"Exactly," Carmen said. "Dom, meet our newest client, Binky Mortimer."

"*Encantado,*" Domingo said, shaking her hand.

Binky flushed. "I love *la vida loca!*"

Domingo looked confused.

"Binky's mother was Venezuelan, and she's on a—how should I put it?—*journey* to explore her Latin roots," Carmen explained.

Domingo shrugged good-naturedly. "Got it. One more thing: virgin *mojitos* all around?"

"You know how we roll," Alicia said.

"Thanks, sweetie," Carmen said.

"*Claro,*" Domingo said, walking away.

"He's cute," Binky said to Carmen. "Speaking of cute, where's Gaz?"

Alicia sighed. "Where he always is—rehearsing with his band or working at the Gap."

Jamie narrowed her eyes. "You know he has to work to help his mother out. We don't all have the luxury of rich parents." Her tone was sharper than she intended, and Alicia took note.

"You don't have to tell me how hard he works," Alicia said. "I just miss him sometimes, that's all."

"Hey, are you guys coming to the Everglades–C. G. High game Wednesday?" Binky asked, changing the subject.

The three friends exchanged glances. None of them was exactly the rah-rah football-game type.

"Uh, we hadn't planned on it," Alicia replied for them all.

"You've *got* to come; I'm a cheerleader, and our new routine is *sick*," Binky pleaded. "Besides, it'll be fun."

"Well," Carmen said, "Domingo is actually a big football fan and had said something about wanting to go. And, like they say, the customer is always right."

"I'll be there," Alicia said.

"I guess that means me, too," Jamie said.

Binky beamed. "You guys are going to love it."

She launched into something about routines and pyramids, giving Jamie a much-needed chance to zone. She looked off into the distance. Had she overreacted with Dash? It wasn't like a boy had never unsnapped her bra before. There had been the guy at Fitzgibbons. He had had a bet with one of his prep-school pals that he could get to second base with her, and Jamie had found out and been heartbroken. But Dash was different. He wasn't a boy, he was a young man, a gentleman, or so she had thought. And the evening had been so . . . so perfect. It just infuriated her that she didn't have enough experience to tell whether the bad was in Dash's court or hers.

Again she wished she could talk to the girls. But even if Binky hadn't been there, she wasn't sure she would have felt comfortable telling Alicia and Carmen the truth. She felt a little like the boy who cried wolf. She'd spent so much time talking about the Bronx and how hard-core she was and how wack the rest of the world was that she'd somewhat lost the ability to talk about feeling vulnerable. And she wasn't sure that if she took the chance and opened up to them her friends would really hear her when she said that she *knew* some guys thought girls from the hood were easy. She had never told them about her past. Was now the time to start?

Jamie was pondering the matter so intensely that she didn't realize that Alicia was trying to get her attention.

"Hello, space cadet," she said, waving a hand. "Talking business here. I met with Padre Hottie, and he's totally cool with doing the *quince* ceremony on the boat. And Carmen had the best idea for the shoe change."

Jamie shook off her sad thoughts and focused.

"After the priest blesses the *quince,* your dad changes your shoes from flats to heels to symbolize your transition to womanhood," Carmen explained to Binky. "What I was thinking was that when you take off your flats, the captain of the yacht could run them up the flagpole. It could be really funny."

Binky shook her head. "Cute, but I haven't worn flats off the tennis court since eighth grade, and I'm not going to start now."

"Are you serious?" Alicia asked. "The changing of the shoes is a critical part of the *quinceañera* ceremony. It's an important part of the tradition."

"Symbolic," Carmen added.

"No can do, *chicas,*" Binky said, tossing her blond hair so it fell perfectly over her sequined one-shouldered top. "Mortimer women don't do flats."

Typical, Jamie thought. Would Dash have been all handsy with a girl from the Mortimers' exclusive West Side Country Club? She didn't think so. Mortimer women didn't do flats, and Mortimer guys didn't have any manners.

But Binky was a client. And Amigas Inc. was a serious business. Jamie was a part of that business, and she had to stay focused. She started to tap at her phone, then pulled up her Style.com app and showed the picture to Binky. "Not even Lanvin ballet flats?"

Binky looked surprised. Then she smiled. "Those I could do."

Nice, Alicia mouthed to Jamie.

Jamie smiled and, for a second, forgot how anxious and humiliated she felt about Dash.

Alicia continued through her checklist. "Carmen. Binky's dress—what are your thoughts?"

Carmen pulled out her notebook. "I was thinking that we could do something really different for Binky. Something that would kind of harken back to another era. You have such a classic look, so sleek and stylish."

"I have always wished I'd grown up in the era of ball gowns and horse-drawn carriages," Binky admitted.

Carmen switched places with Alicia in the booth so that she could sit next to Binky. "Well, I wasn't going back in time as far as horse-drawn carriages," she said, "but every time I look at you, all I think of is pictures from the Jazz Age. The nineteen twenties. So, what I've designed is a twenty-first century take on something from that era. Take a look while I quickly get some measurements."

Binky stood up and took the sketchbook. She silently flipped through the sketches as Carmen moved around her with a measuring tape. The drawings made Binky even taller and thinner than she already was. And the dress: there must have been a dozen sketches of it, and it was to die for. Floor-length, with a fish-tail skirt. A ballerina neckline with ruffled details, princess seams. It was an Oscars show dress. It was a "Girl, you're a woman now" dress. And the color, a perfect tangerine, with a pink lining, was bright but elegant at the same time. Binky, who had turned shopping into an Olympic sport and had easily owned hundreds of dresses in her lifetime, was speechless.

"You don't like it?" Carmen said, panicking. "I thought orange was your favorite, but it's easy for me to sketch it in another color if you want."

"No, that's not it," Binky said.

"It's too long," Carmen said. "You don't do long, I've noticed. I'm so sorry."

Binky shook her head. "No, I love it. I love it."

She gave Carmen a huge hug, and then, still holding on to her tightly, she burst into tears.

"I'm flattered, really," Carmen said, embracing the sobbing girl and shooting the others a worried glance. "But it's just a dress. Exquisitely designed. Project Runway–worthy. Someday I'll rule the fashion-world frock. But really, it's just a dress."

"For real," Jamie muttered.

Binky sniffed. For the first time since they'd met her, she looked less like a debutante and more like a regular teen. "It's not just the quality of the dress. I never told you guys why orange was my favorite color," she said, reaching into her purse to withdraw a photo.

"This is my favorite picture of my mom," Binky explained, holding it close to her heart. "She was Miss Venezuela; then she went to Montreal for the Miss Universe competition, and that's where she met my dad." She held up the photo. "Look at what she wore for the evening gown competition."

The dress was dated, but there was no way to deny that it was a distant relative of the dress that Carmen had envisioned. Binky's mother was the picture of *belleza* in a strapless tangerine gown with a big navy bow and a fish-tail hem.

"That's just spooky," Alicia said after a moment of hushed silence.

"And pretty amazing," Binky added. "My mom won't be there, really, but I don't know—somehow, this dress is a sign. Like I'm doing what she would have wanted and she's smiling down on me."

"Sometimes, things are just meant to be," Carmen said softly. "I'm happy you're happy. I just hope that I can make it as beautiful as the sketch, and as beautiful as your mother's picture. I'll buy the fabric today. Can you come to my house on Wednesday before the game for another fitting?"

"You live in one of those little bitty houses on the canal, right?" Binky said, snapping back to her usual chipper self. "I've always wanted to see what they were like inside. It must be like living in a gingerbread house. So tiny!"

Alicia and Jamie worried that Carmen would bristle at Binky's comment, but their friend held it together.

"Here's the address." Carmen calmly handed Binky a slip of paper.

"Awesome," Binky said, getting up and giving them all hugs. "I'd better go. My driver will be waiting, but I'm excited. I can't believe you designed a dress that's so much like my mother. I love you for that, Carmen."

After she left, the *amigas* exchanged perplexed glances.

"She's so hard to figure out," Alicia said.

"One minute, she's *completamente* stuck-up . . ." Jamie said.

"And the next, she's as sweet as can be," Carmen said, completing her thought.

Their business done, Alicia asked Domingo for the check. He shook his head. "Today's lunch is on me."

"But we can take it out of the budget," Alicia said. "And believe me, the budget on this particular *quince* is really generous."

Domingo smiled, and Carmen nearly melted. He was no Padre Alfonso—he was better.

"I may not have the Mortimer cash, but I can treat my girlfriend and her friends to lunch every once in a while," Domingo said, leaning over to kiss Carmen on the forehead. "I'll see you later, right? You're coming to my house for dinner."

"Wouldn't miss it," Carmen said. "*Gracias.*"

Alicia and Carmen called out their thanks, and Domingo returned to waiting on his tables. Even at three in the afternoon, the Bongos lunch crowd was hopping.

"Hey, on the topic of cute, nice guys," Alicia said, turning to look at Jamie, "you seemed to be having a really nice time with Dash."

"It wasn't that nice a time, really. More of a bust," Jamie mumbled, slurping her watered-down Coke.

"Why?" Carmen asked. "He's a great dancer, super-charming, and, most importantly, really into you."

Jamie took a deep breath. She had to say something. And the truth seemed the best option. "Yeah," she said. "He was so into me that when he drove me home, after he kissed me good night, he tried to take my bra off."

She could feel the tears coming, the ones she'd been fighting back all day. "The best date of my entire life ruined by the fact that Mr. Moneybags thinks he can go extra far with the girl from the South Bronx."

Carmen, always the voice of reason, rested a hand on Jamie's arm. "I don't want to discount what you're feeling, sweetie, but are you sure that's what Dash was thinking? Sometimes in the heat of the moment, guys push the limit. . . ."

Jamie's tears vanished instantly. Her eyes flashed, and her voice trembled with rage. "So, if a guy gets all hot and bothered, that's *my* problem? Something *I've* got to deal with?"

Carmen shook her head. "No, that's not what I'm saying. I'm just saying that he seems like a nice guy. Maybe the two of you should talk about it before you completely write it off."

Jamie stood up. "You know what? I don't want to talk about it. I never wanted to talk about it. In fact, I'm done talking about it. Let's pretend it never happened, okay?"

Then, grabbing her things, she ran out of the restaurant, leaving her very confused friends behind.

• • •

Hoping to get her mind off Dash, Jamie decided to work on her own *quinceañera* checklist. But after a run to the party supply store to get bottles and then a quick stop at the craft shop to pick up mini seashells for Binky's message-in-a-bottle *quince* invitations, Jamie went home still thinking of him. Her father was sitting at the kitchen table when she walked in.

"Hola, Papá," she said, kissing him on the cheek.

It was rare for Davide Sosa to be home. Jamie's father worked so many long hours at the car service she sometimes felt as though he lived in a different city and that he just came back to be with Jamie and her mother on the weekends.

"Anything you want to tell me?" her father asked, looking up from the paper he was reading. He raised an eyebrow, attempting to be subtle. It didn't work.

Jamie cocked her head to one side and observed her father. He still looked much younger than his 50-some years. When she had been at Fitzgibbons Academy, the girls there had said that he looked like Antonio Banderas, and while there was much about which she wouldn't have agreed with them, on this she did.

"Papa, what do you mean?" she asked, growing concerned. "Where's Mom? What would I have to tell you?"

"Your mother is fine. She went out for coffee with her friend Tasha."

"So, if she's okay and you're okay, what's up?" Jamie asked.

"You should go to your room," her father replied.

Now Jamie was really confused. "Am I grounded? What did I do? I was out last night, but I texted Mom and she said it was okay."

"Go to your room, Jamie," her father repeated.

Sighing, Jamie turned and left the kitchen. She walked down the hall with a nervous feeling in her stomach.

Opening the door to her room, she smelled them before she saw them. Dozens upon dozens of roses. All different colors: lavender, red, orange, hot pink. All in different vases. Each with the same note: *Discúlpame, discúlpame, discúlpame, discúlpame, discúlpame—Forgive me, forgive me, forgive me—Dash.*

After she got over the shock, she took a picture with her phone. Quickly, she typed a message: *Can you believe this guy?*

Then she hit send. She couldn't imagine what Alicia would say when she saw that Jamie's bedroom had been transformed into a flower shop.

A few minutes later, there was a reply: *Hard to tell*

from the pix. Romantic, over the top, or stalkerish?

Jamie smiled and typed back: *Borderline OTT, but still pretty romantic.*

Ten seconds later, there was a new message: *He seems sorry. I think he really likes you. So . . . do you like him?*

Jamie sat back on her bed. She traced the pattern of her Giant Robot sheets, special edition from Japan. Did she like Dash? Yes. Was she still mad at him for acting like a hyperactive jock? Yes. She typed back: *Can you like someone and be mad at them at the same time?*

The answer came quickly: *Happens.*

Jamie kicked off her sneakers and crossed her legs. She looked around and took in the dozens of bouquets. She'd never seen anything more beautiful, or been in a room that smelled sweeter. Did the rooms at the Mortimer house, scented by such expensive roses, smell this sweet all the time? And if she said, "Okay, I forgive you," after Dash sent her so many flowers, would it mean she was being swayed by him—or by his money? She took out her phone and typed another message to her best friend: *Do you think he's trying to buy me off with such an expensive gift? Or is he really sorry?*

Not even one minute later, the reply came: *I think he's really sorry.*

Just then the land line rang, startling Jamie. For a moment, she allowed herself to think that it was Dash—although, in the great game of Whose Turn Is It? the ball was now most definitely in her court. She'd stomped off, furious. He'd sent her a truckload of roses. Now it was on her to call him and let him know whether or not she accepted his apology.

She could hear her father answer the phone in the cheesy way he always did when one of her girlfriends called. It was probably Carmen, with some *quince* business. She ran out of her room and opened the door to the living room just as her father said the punchline of his favorite joke.

"The doctor was a woman!" he bellowed into the phone.

"Hey, Papa," Jamie said, interrupting him before he could start a new one. "Is it for me?"

"Is it a day that ends with a *Y*?" her father asked, handing her the phone. "It's Alicia."

Jamie smiled. "Thanks. Can I have a minute?"

"So, Lici, do you think I should forgive him?" she said, when her dad had left the room.

"Dash?" Alicia asked.

"Who else?" Jamie said. "I'm glad you called. You have to come over. Photos do not do these flowers justice, and the smell, *niña*. These roses put even the fanciest perfume to shame."

"Dash sent you flowers?" Alicia asked. "*Qué caballero.* Very sweet."

Jamie suddenly had a sinking feeling in the pit of her stomach. "Lici, we've been texting about this for the past twenty minutes."

Alicia sounded confused. "But I was in the pool. I just came in."

The sinking feeling got worse. This didn't make any sense.

Jamie didn't get it. Alicia was many things, but absent-minded was most definitely not one of them. Nor cruel. She would never have played a practical joke. Would she?

"I texted you a picture of the gajillion roses that Dash sent me as soon as I got home," Jamie said.

"I never got any picture."

Jamie gulped. "Let me call you back."

She hung up and scrolled back through her text messages. Suddenly, she let out a squeak. How could she have made such a junior high school texting mistake?

Alicia and Dash's phone numbers had the same first six digits. At a quick glance, she'd mistaken Dash's number for her friend's. She'd sent *him* a picture of the flowers that he'd sent her. She'd told *him* how much she liked him and asked *him* whether he thought that the expensive gift was in poor taste.

What was she going to do? Jamie weighed her options: Lose her phone? Not such a good idea, because phones were expensive. Pretend to have lost her phone and when she saw Dash again, if he mentioned the text messages, say, "Oh, I lost my phone *weeks* ago"?

It occurred to her that while it was indeed a juvenile thing to text with abandon and without checking to make sure you had the right phone number, she wasn't the only guilty party. Dash must've known that she *hadn't* known she was texting him. He had played her. Again.

But this time, she was far from angry. He liked her. He'd not only sent her a flotilla of roses to say so, he'd gotten her text messages and asked, pretty blatantly, if she were in the forgiving mood. And wouldn't you know it? She was.

She picked up the land line and dialed his number.

"Hey, *querida*," he said softly.

"Hay is for horses," Jamie answered.

"Right," he said, laughing.

"So, are you, like, the Batman of text messages?"

she asked. "Sending messages without ever revealing your identity?"

"Am I in trouble again?" he asked.

Jamie waited a moment before answering to let him sweat just a little. "No, you're not. Thank you for the flowers."

"Do you like roses?" Dash asked eagerly. "I know they are a little bit of a cliché, but I love the smell of real garden roses."

Jamie smiled and took a deep breath. "Now I do, too."

"Go out with me again," Dash asked. "Give me the chance to show that I can be a perfect gentleman."

"Well, your sister has convinced us all to go to the C. G.–Everglades football game tomorrow," Jamie said.

"Me, too," Dash answered. "Should we go together?"

Jamie had held on to one of the cards that had come with the roses. Now she began to doodle on the back of it. "Not so fast, cowboy. *Maybe* I'll see you there. And *maybe* there'll be a seat next to me, and *maybe* if you sit down, I won't get up and move to another bleacher seat. But I'm not making any promises."

"No promises necessary. I'll be there," Dash said. "And Jamie, I'm really sorry."

"Good night, Dash," Jamie said, hanging up.

She put the phone back on its base in the hallway. Her cell phone immediately started to beep. The message read: *Dulces sueños.*

She kissed the phone as if she were thirteen again. Sweet dreams to you, too, Dash, she thought.

CHAPTER 8

ON WEDNESDAY, right on schedule, Binky arrived at Carmen's family home for her fitting. Carmen's family lived on the Canals, a cool, artsy, residential section of one of Miami's oldest neighborhoods.

When Carmen opened the front door, Binky gave her new friend an air kiss on both cheeks and then moaned dramatically.

"You should have warned me that I was going to the hinterlands," she said.

As the two girls stood together in the foyer, Carmen quickly picked up on the fact that Binky wasn't her usual chipper self. Looking around, she tried to figure out why.

Carmen lived in the two-story Craftsman house with her older sister, Una; her brother, Tino; and her three younger stepsisters. Christian, her British step-father, taught history at Florida International University, and Sophia, her mother, was the head of the math department at C. G. High. Javier Ruben, her Jewish Argentinean father, produced *telenovelas*, and Natalia, her stepmother, starred in them. Binky might have been a teenage diva, but with her crazy family, Carmen was used to the dramatic.

"What's the problem, Binky?" Carmen asked now, leading the other girl into the kitchen. "Can I get you something to drink?"

Binky sighed, as though the question were deeply perplexing. "Voss. Sparkling. With a twist of lime."

Carmen opened the fridge and shook her head. "No can do, B. How about Pellegrino sparkling? With a twist of lemon?"

"Acceptable," Binky said, taking a seat at the kitchen counter. "What is *not* acceptable," she went on, answering Carmen's earlier question, "is the two-mile hike I had to do just to get to your house. You could have told me they don't allow cars on your teeny-tiny street."

Ah, so this was what was bothering the princess. "That's the beauty of living on the Canals!" Carmen said, handing Binky her water. "When I was a kid, we were always allowed to ride our bikes all along the towpath, because there was no danger of cars."

"But I had to slog over here from the lot. It took *hours,* and I'm wearing *heels,*" Binky sighed, feigning exhaustion. She lifted one foot and rotated it. By now, Carmen was used to the fact that Binky, while sweet, was the living definition of "OTT."

"It takes about five minutes, ten at a turtle's pace," said Carmen. She looked down at the high heels on Binky's feet. They had to be at least three and a half inches tall. "Next time, do what we do. Wear flip-flops for the walk, and change when you get here."

"Ha!" Binky said. "Like there'll be a next time. If we need to do additional fittings, we'll do them in the civilized part of town: my house."

Just then, the front door slammed, and Tino ambled in. He was dressed in a sweaty soccer uniform, and judging by the amount of dirt on his cleats and his previously white socks, he'd just come from practice. His curly dark hair was sopping wet and fell in Botticelli curls across his forehead.

"What's up?" Tino asked as he dribbled his soccer ball into the kitchen. His eyes on the ball, he didn't notice the visitor.

"Um, your funk, that's what's up," Carmen said, wrinkling her nose.

Tino smiled. "Good honest sweat. I earned it. I'm

proud of it. Give me a hug, sis." He ran over to Carmen and made as if to pull her into a big bear hug. She squealed and jumped away.

"Come on, Binky. Let's find a less Hazmat-worthy zone of the house," Carmen said.

Binky, however, was not going anywhere. She appeared glued to her chair.

"Hi, I'm Bianca," she said, reaching out to shake Tino's hand.

Carmen looked surprised. She'd never heard Binky use her given name before.

Tino smiled. "Pleased to meet you," he said pleasantly. "I would shake your hand, but as my sister has made abundantly clear, I'm filthy."

Binky kept her hand outstretched. "That's okay. I'm in the sweat business, too."

Tino narrowed his eyes as he took a swig from the bottle of Gatorade he had just opened. "You play soccer, too?"

Binky giggled flirtatiously. "Not exactly. I'm a cheerleader."

"Oh, gotcha. That's cool," Tino said, nodding. "Cheerleading is definitely a sport."

Carmen had been watching the entire exchange with quiet interest. Wait till she told the others about the heavy-duty flirting happening in her own kitchen! But that would have to come later. The clock was ticking. "Hey, Binky, we should really get going with this fitting. You have a game to get to, and I've got a ton of work to do on your dress. I want it to be perfect."

Binky finally rose, reluctantly, from her chair. "Yeah, um, can't wait to see it. Nice meeting you, Tino."

"You, too, Bianca," Tino said.

"Come with me to my atelier," Carmen said. Responding to Binky's confused look, she added, "Also known as the room I share with my sister."

Binky followed her up the stairs. "Your house is so tiny and cute," she said, having apparently recovered from her initial displeasure with the location. Carmen had to wonder if this had anything to do with a certain soccer-playing brother. "After I graduate from college, I could totally see living in a funky little house like this one," Binky continued. "It's one of those down-to-earth experiences that everyone should have."

Carmen smiled patiently. This rich-girl's-view-of-the-world monologue was not unexpected, coming from Binky. They'd all heard similar ones before over the past few days. The best thing to do was just go with the flow. Binky really didn't mean any harm.

"These are nice," Binky said as they moved through

the hall. She was gazing at the black-and-white family photos lining the walls. "Who took them?"

"My stepfather. He's a complete photography nut."

"That's funny," Binky said. "My dad is the complete opposite. I don't know if it's because my mom passed away, but he never wants old photos around; he says it's a waste of time to live in the past and that the future belongs to those who live in the present."

"He sounds like he's in a lot of pain," Carmen observed.

"Well, he *is* married to my stepmother," Binky said, shrugging dismissively.

"I've got a stepmother, too," Carmen said. "Mine's a *telenovela* star. Nice enough, but a diva all the way."

"My stepmother, Bev, is more like Glenn Close in *101 Dalmatians*," Binky said. "She's stylish, cold—and I'm pretty sure that, if she could, she'd be mean to puppies. Luckily I'm allergic, so we can't have any to test the theory."

Carmen laughed. "I'll make sure to stay out of her way."

Binky stopped in front of one of the pictures. It was a large, silver-framed photograph of Carmen's mother in a graduation cap and gown.

"I would love to have some photographs of my

mother around the house," Binky said softly, her finger tracing the frame.

"You should ask your dad," Carmen said. "Tell him how much it means to you."

"You think I haven't?" Binky asked. "Every time I bring it up, he hands me a wad of cash and tells me to buy myself something nice."

"So, bring it up again," Carmen suggested.

Binky shook her head. "After a while you just get tired of hearing the word *no*." Turning away from the photo, she cocked her head. "So, are we going to do this? My dress won't make itself." All traces of the sadness that had just moments ago enveloped her were gone.

Carmen knew better than to push. People grieved and dealt with things in their own ways. She continued down the hall and turned in to the tiny room she shared with her older sister. Binky followed and sat down in the desk chair.

"After I got your measurements, I started working on your dress right away. I stayed up all night sewing," Carmen said, walking over to her closet. "I think this is one of my best creations yet. Try it on." She pulled out a mass of tangerine silk and handed it to Binky. "Be careful; there are lots and lots of pins." Moments later,

Binky stood in front of the full-length mirror wearing the dress. Her eyes were gleaming. "I know it's not done," she whispered, "but I'll wear it just like this. Pins and all."

While Alicia and Jamie were naturally stylish and always looked well put together, Carmen had a special gift. She knew exactly what the best look was for all of their *quince* clients. Even if it was a color or a cut they'd never worn before, they looked at themselves wearing Carmen's creations and saw their prettiest selves. Binky was a case in point.

Carmen laughed at the other girl's rapt expression. "I'm glad you like it, but the whole right side still needs to be sewn, *chica*."

Binky shook her head. "You can't make me take it off. I love it too much!"

Carmen put her hand on her hip. "Don't make me have to count to ten, like I do with my little sisters."

Binky sighed. "Fine, fine. But at least snap a picture with your phone, so I can stare at it in my free time."

This was something Carmen could agree to. She grabbed her phone and took the picture. "Okay, *chica*, take it off. And maybe don't share the photo. We want this to be a surprise."

Binky plopped onto the bed—it was Una's bed, as

the older sibling had claimed bottom bunk years before. "Fine with me. I don't want all the other girls to be rocking couture, anyway."

Carmen couldn't help smiling at the word *couture*. It was her dream to have her own line of clothing one day. Even though creating a single dress for Bianca Mortimer hardly constituted a fashion launch, it made her feel good that her original designs were prized by clients who obviously knew quality when they saw it.

"I've done some scouting," Carmen said, "and I think these maxidresses would be perfect for your *damas*. The navy with orange accents will totally complement your dress and not take away from it."

Carmen pulled up pictures of the dresses she had researched on her phone and showed Binky.

"Perfect, I love them," Binky said.

"I'm glad. So, am I ever going to get to meet the girls in your court?" Carmen asked. "Remind me who they are again."

"You'll meet them soon. Let's see, there are a few girls from my cheerleading squad; my best friend from tennis camp; and my cousin, Lily Mortimer. Though how we're going to tear her away from her annual Thanksgiving ski trip to Vail is beyond me." Binky tossed her long blond hair over her shoulder.

"I'm sure she'll show up," Carmen said encouragingly.

"Yeah, well, Lily is a fanatical snow bunny. Its hard for anything or anybody to drag her away from the slopes," Binky said. "So we'll see."

Carmen changed the subject to that of the *chambelanes* and asked Binky who the guys in her court were going to be. She wanted a good visual while figuring out what they would wear.

"My brother, Dash, of course," Binky said, beginning to list them. "His friend, Troy, whom you've met."

"He's the one who thinks he's so charming but has no game, right?" Carmen said.

Binky nodded. "He's a little bit of a player— wannabe player, I should say—but we've known Troy since we were little kids. Deep down, he's a good guy."

"Okay, I'm going to have to take your word for that," Carmen teased. "But what about *your* date? *Your chambelán*? A lot of girls just take their cousin if they think their parents aren't going to approve of the guy they *really* like."

Binky let out one of her trademark overdramatic sighs. "That's just the problem. There isn't a guy that I like. Don't laugh, but I was dating this archduke sort of guy from Austria. How could I even begin to envision spending my life, or even attending senior prom, with a guy who got me a bratwurst cookbook for my birthday? But anyway, his family eventually moved back to Austria, and we were never that serious in any case."

Carmen let out a loud laugh. "You're kidding about the cookbook, right?"

Binky shook her head. "I wish." She paused, as though she had just had an idea. "What about your brother?"

"Tino?"

"He's cute," Binky said, clasping her hands together in apparent growing excitement over her idea. "Is he seeing someone?"

"Outside of his soccer ball?" Carmen said. "I don't think so."

Binky looked suddenly shy, an expression Carmen rarely if ever saw on her face. "Do you think he would be my *chambelán*? Will you ask him?" Binky asked.

This was a pretty big favor. On one hand, Carmen was pretty confident that he would say yes. Binky was cute, and Tino was always up for a party. On the other hand, if things didn't go well—and that was always a possibility—Carmen would probably never hear the end of it.

Binky cleared her throat, waiting for an answer.

"Sure," Carmen said finally, giving in. She hoped she hadn't just made a big mistake.

After Binky left to get ready for the game, Carmen went to find her brother.

She knocked on the door of his room, where she found him attempting to pull off an octopuslike juggling act of playing Madden, drinking a milk shake, and kicking his soccer ball from foot to foot.

There was no sense in beating around the bush. Tino was a get-to-the-point kind of guy. So she asked him straight out if he would be Binky's *chambelán*. The grin that spread across his face was the answer she needed. But of course, he had to say something.

"So, she's crushing on me, huh?" Tino asked. He sounded pleased by the idea. The only times Carmen ever usually heard him sound like that was when he was talking about soccer. "Who could blame her? I've got mad skills."

He picked up the soccer ball and began bouncing it from ankle to ankle and then knee to knee.

"Do you think she'd like me to do this? Or this? Or how about this?"

Carmen tsk-tsked. "I think she'd like you to put on a tux and be a good *chambelán*."

Tino stopped bouncing the ball. "That I can do."

"Thanks! I'll tell her," Carmen said.

As she turned to leave, Tino called out, "Hey, sis!"

Carmen looked back at him. "Yeah?"

"Um, thanks for the intro," Tino said bashfully.

Back in her room, she felt the urge to share this new development. She picked up the phone to call Jamie. Then she changed her mind and hung up. Then she picked the phone back up and redialed.

"Hey, Jamie," she said when her friend answered. "Want to hear something interesting? Binky asked me to ask Tino to be to her *chambelán*."

"What?" Jamie yelped. "Miss Head Cheerleader doesn't have a boyfriend?"

"Well, she did, but the archduke moved back to Austria with his family."

"Of course he did," Jamie said.

"Anyway, I asked Tino, and even though I thought for sure he would say no, he said yes!"

"That's weird."

"*Guys* are weird," Carmen said. Then, realizing she could use this to try to get some thoughts out of Jamie on Dash, she added, "And kinda stupid. But not all of them. I honestly believe that Dash is less weird and less stupid than most. He likes you, you like him. Give him another chance, J."

For a moment, there was just silence, and Carmen wondered if she'd pushed too hard. But then Jamie said, "I can do that," and filled her friend in on the flowers and on the texts she'd accidentally sent to Dash.

"My mom always says there are no accidents," Carmen said when Jamie had finished. "Everything happens for a reason."

"And the reason for this is . . . ?" Jamie asked.

"He's probably the only guy in Miami cool enough to go out with you, Jamie-James," Carmen teased.

CHAPTER 9

LATER THAT afternoon, the Coral Gables football team played Everglades Academy, Binky and Dash's school. The rivalry between the schools was nothing short of intense.

Of course, with such strong rivalry came strong rules, which weren't supposed to be broken—such as fraternizing with the other side. But Binky didn't care. Dressed in her green and white cheerleader uniform, she went running over to Alicia and her crew as soon as they arrived, shouting, *"Amigas!* Wassup?"

The girls exchanged the now familiar hugs and then, just as quickly as she had come, Binky went back to join her squad. After completing a series of acrobatic moves, the Everglades girls started to cheer.

E is for Excellence,
E is for Elite,

But E is not for Everybody,
Because E can't be beat.

The three female members of Amigas Inc. sat in the bleachers on the Coral Gables side, passing a thermos of hot chocolate back and forth and watching the cheerleaders. It wasn't snowing, but even in Miami, wintertime could be a little chilly. Or at least they liked to think so, since it gave them an excuse to drink hot cocoa.

"I think I would rather walk over a bed of hot coals than be a cheerleader," Jamie declared as she watched.

"Don't hate, appreciate," Alicia insisted. "Look at Binky flip. She's really good."

Just then, Gaz ambled up through the bleachers toward them.

"I have to say that if it takes Binky Mortimer to get you girls out to a football game, then she's okay with me," Gaz said after he had taken a seat.

Alicia gave him a playful nudge and slid her hand into his. She couldn't really argue with him. He was always trying to get her to go to games—he was a football fan in spite of his more artsy side—and she was always saying no. But when Binky said jump, you had to ask how high. As they watched the heavily uniformed players pass—and more often drop—the football, Alicia found herself hoping Gaz didn't think this would become a regular thing.

"So, what's up with you and Dash?" Alicia asked Jamie when she got too bored to watch the game anymore. "Everything cool now?"

Jamie looked down at her hands. "We talked, so I guess it's sort of cool. But I don't know, Lici. We're just so different, and I've had some experience with 'different.' It doesn't tend to work out for me."

"I think you and Dash have more in common than you think," Alicia observed. "You're both stylish. You're both amazing dancers. You both have a passion for Latin culture, and you're both really, really good at what you do."

"Dash is an amazing golf player," she added when Jamie still didn't say anything. "Binky says he's good enough to go pro."

"Of course she'd say that," Jamie finally said.

"It's not just her," said Domingo, who had joined them to watch the game and overheard. "Check this out."

He handed Jamie a copy of *Miami Golf* magazine. On the cover was a picture of Dash, looking sweeter and handsomer than any heartbreaker had any right to look.

The cover headline read: *Hey, Miami, meet the future of American golf!*

"Wow," said Alicia.

"Impressive," Gaz agreed.

Jamie was silent. Finally she got up and said, "I'm going to get a hot dog. Anyone hungry?" At a nod from Gaz, she began to make her way down the bleachers.

Gaz followed. "Hey, I'm not trying to get all in your business—" he told her when they were away from the others.

"But . . ." Jamie said.

It had taken some time for Gaz and Alicia to work out their secret undercover crushing on each other and finally start dating. But in the process, Gaz and Jamie had developed an easy rapport. Alicia's family was well off. Carmen's family was financially comfortable. Gaz and Jamie had bonded over the fact that, by contrast, they had grown up knowing that a new school year meant one new pair of shoes and one new pair of jeans—not five or six. When Jamie got impatient with her *amigas* or one of their spoiled clients, it was Gaz who was able to talk her down.

Now it seemed he was going to try to do so again. But he didn't launch into anything right away.

They ordered food and drinks for themselves and their friends. Gaz paid and they began to walk back to the bleachers.

Finally, he spoke. "Don't be mad, but Alicia told me what happened." He held up a hand as she started to protest. "Just take it from me, J. As a guy who's said and done more than his share of stupid things, when you give a guy a second chance, if he's good and if he's smart, he won't waste it. And, James? Dash is good. And smart."

The game was a close one for a while, and even Jamie forgot her preoccupations and got caught up in the excitement, so much so that she completely forgot that Dash had said he'd be coming to the game—until the C. G. quarterback scored a touchdown that tied the game, the crowd went wild, and Jamie looked up . . . to see him standing there.

"Hey, is this seat taken?" he asked. He was dressed in a charcoal gray cashmere turtleneck, navy blazer, and jeans, and he looked like a long, lean slice of handsome.

"I haven't decided yet," Jamie teased, Gaz's words echoing in her mind. *Second chances . . . second chances . . .*

She had dressed carefully for the game in cropped

jeans, which she'd studded at the ankle herself; a vintage leopard-print blouse; and a tweed jacket that had belonged to her grandfather. Her leather booties— an eBay score—provided the finishing touch to what was quickly becoming one of her favorite outfits. She'd always found that being dressed to the nines was the easiest way to quiet her nerves, but, in such close proximity to Dash, and knowing who he was and what he represented, she found that her fierce and fabulous outfit didn't feel like nearly enough.

"Well, how about we try this?" Dash asked sweetly. "I'll sit down, and I'll start talking, and if the very sight of me is repulsive to you, then feel free to tell me to leave at any time."

"You've got yourself a deal," Jamie said, sliding over and making room for him on the bleachers.

"So, what's the score?" Dash asked when he was settled, his knee just brushing Jamie's. She debated moving slightly away but decided against it. The feeling was nice. Warm. Comforting.

"Score? They actually keep track of that kind of thing?" Jamie answered, pretending to look shocked. "Honestly, I have no idea what's going on. Who's who, what's what? To me, it's just a bunch of big guys running around in tight pants."

Dash let out a loud laugh, causing the rest of the group to turn and look, curious. When he didn't explain but instead just kept looking at Jamie, they shrugged and went back to watching the game, happy to ignore the pair. Dash, meanwhile, had no real interest in the game himself. "Are you saying you prefer a sport with men in looser pants? Khakis, perhaps? And a nice, clean, crisp polo?" He winked.

"Oh, my gosh, you just know me so well, Dash Mortimer!" Jamie exclaimed, holding a hand to her heart as though she were impressed. Then she narrowed her eyes and grinned mischievously. "More like, I don't like sports. Period."

"I guess I'll have to do something about that, then, won't I?" he said, reaching out to take her hand. She stiffened and pulled away, causing his eyes to fill with regret.

"Look, Jamie, I can understand why you thought my coming on so hot and heavy was a sign of disrespect for you," Dash said. "But I swear that I have nothing but the utmost respect for you."

"So why act like such a jerk after such a great date?" Jamie asked.

"You're a painter, right?" Dash said.

Jamie nodded, puzzled.

"Are you ever in the middle of a painting and your hand starts to move and you look at the canvas and you go, whoa, what is that?"

"All the time," she replied.

"Well, that's kind of like what happened to me," Dash said. "All I was thinking about was kissing you, but my hands were way ahead of my brain. I'm truly sorry. I promise never to do it again."

For a moment, she said nothing. She just stared out at the field, her mind whirling. What he said made sense. And it was honest. She owed it to him to be honest, too. "Look, Dash, I don't know what it is about you, but I really like you," she finally said. "You should consider yourself lucky, because I really don't like that many people. But now that you know how I feel, I don't need you to make me any promises about the future or anything. I just need for you to treat me with respect in the here and now."

"That's something I can do. . . . Would it be respectful, for example, if I *asked* to kiss you right now?" Dash whispered.

"Public place, bright lights," Jamie said, looking around. "It should be fine."

Dash kissed her softly and pulled away.

"Was that okay?" he asked.

"That was perfect."

She leaned forward to kiss him again, but they were interrupted by Binky. Apparently, while they had been talking, the game had finally ended. Binky had her hands on her hips and a big smile on her face. "It's very nice to see that you two have made up. But now, can we get back to more pressing matters—like my *quince*?"

CHAPTER 10

WHILE BINKY thought it perfectly acceptable to put up a romantic roadblock for Dash and Jamie, her *quinceañera* was not going to get in the way of her own love life—or her attempt at one.

That Friday night, Binky and Tino met up for their first official date, to see if the *chambelán* idea would even work. They'd been talking and texting nonstop since the day before.

Because Tino didn't have a car, Binky did the modern-girl thing—well, the modified modern-girl thing—and picked him up in the family car. The person driving was her father's chauffeur, Ferris.

"Nice wheels," Tino said when he climbed into the backseat.

He'd dressed for the date in a carefully ironed shirt with French cuffs and cuff links that he'd borrowed from his stepfather. Binky had stepped up her look, too—in a navy blue sweater dress with a thin gold chain and cobalt blue satin platform pumps.

"You look great," Tino said.

"Thanks." Binky tossed her blond hair casually. It was in fact a not so casual move that she practiced in the mirror a dozen times a day.

Tino sat next to her, buckled his seat belt, and stretched his legs. He was already six feet tall, and legroom was always an issue. But not in the Mortimers' car.

"This is so spacious," he said, admiring the car's interior.

"Glad you like it. So, where should we go for dinner?" Binky asked.

"Your choice," Tino answered. "I hit my savings account this afternoon, so I've got plenty of green."

Binky smiled. "Ooooh! A splurge. Well, in that case, let's go to Lechuga."

In the front, Ferris cleared his throat, trying to get her attention. Binky ignored him.

"Okay with me," Tino said.

Ferris cleared his throat even louder.

"Lechuga, Ferris!" Binky shouted. "And pop a cough drop, you're distracting us."

Ferris eyed Binky in the rearview mirror. "Are

you sure that Lechuga is the most *appropriate* choice, ma'am?" he asked.

Binky, oblivious of the warning tone in his voice, replied, "It's my favorite restaurant. Of course it's appropriate. Let's go."

Sighing, Ferris started the car and headed away from the Canals toward South Beach. It was going to be an interesting night.

From the moment they walked into the restaurant, Tino could feel his appetite waning and his wallet shrinking. The decor was "rustic contemporary," which meant huge, elaborate wooden chandeliers hanging from the ceiling and animals' heads mounted lodge style on the walls. Everyone in the restaurant appeared to be at least the age of Tino's and Binky's parents, and many of them sat squarely in grandparent territory. Looking around, Tino wondered what Binky liked about the place. She seemed too . . . well, alive for it.

The maître d' recognized Binky right away and seated them at a table for two in the middle of the dining room. Hemmed in by the tables all around them, Tino started to feel claustrophobic. He took a deep breath and tried to stay calm.

And then he looked at the menu.

The double-digit figures next to every item were so jarring he felt sure he must have been experiencing vision problems. It had happened to him more than once when he fell hard during a soccer game. It had never happened before in a restaurant, though. Tino decided to level with Binky.

"You do know I'm in the eleventh grade," he said.

"I *adore* older men," Binky replied, batting her eyelashes playfully.

"What I'm trying to say is that this place is expensive," Tino said.

Binky shrugged. "That's why God invented credit cards."

Tino laughed, then grew serious again. "No, that's actually not true. Binky, let me take you to someplace I think you'll like. Someplace I can actually afford without robbing my college fund."

Binky looked hesistant, but finally said, "Okay. I'm game."

Tino dropped twenty dollars on the table for the waiter, and they left. "Most expensive glass of water I've ever had," he mumbled on his way out.

Half an hour later, the two stood on a street corner in the Gables, looking out at the beach. At some point during the drive over, Tino had effortlessly linked hands with Binky, as if it were something he always did. While she had dreamed of being a real-life princess one day, she hadn't felt half the sparks with the archduke that she now felt with Tino Ramirez-Ruben of Miami.

"So, where's the restaurant?" she asked, trying to stay focused. "This is new Prada that I'm rocking, and I don't want to waste it."

"Well, I think you look amazing," Tino said.

"Then this dress is definitely not wasted," Binky replied.

"And don't worry, because . . . we're here." Tino pointed to a food truck parked on the street behind them. "It's called Panini. They make pressed sandwiches, and they're so popular they just Tweet their location and people line up for hours."

"We're having our first date at a food truck?" Binky asked, her eyes wide. "You're kidding, right?" She was making an effort to be more down-to-earth, but earth—when it came to money—wasn't anything she was used to.

Tino put an arm around her. "I'm not kidding, *cariño*. In fact, if you don't like it, then next week I will take you back to the money pit we were just at. I'll treat you to an appetizer—which is really all I can afford there. And I'll drink some more of that expensive water."

"You're on," Binky said, laughing.

When it was their turn to order, Tino looked so cute and so excited it was all Binky could do not to throw her arms around him and kiss him.

"So, what will it be?" Tino asked.

Binky perused the menu. The choices, she had to admit, looked pretty yummy.

"I'll have the citrus-marinated steak panini, with black-bean salsa, Swiss, and pickles," she said.

"An excellent choice," Tino said. "I'll have the same thing."

After they got their dinner, they went and sat on a bench looking out over the beach and started to eat. For a while the only sound came from the distant surf and the sound of chewing.

"Isn't it funny," Tino asked, breaking the silence, "how you can be talking nonstop and then some delicious food arrives, and all of a sudden, *nada*—just pure silence?"

Binky pointed to her full mouth and nodded.

"That was good," she said, when she'd finished chowing down.

"I'm glad you liked it," Tino said.

"Thank you," she said sincerely. "I would never have known about it if you hadn't pulled me out of my fancy place."

"It's my pleasure. After all, aren't you trying to get in touch with your Latina roots? What better way than with me as a tour guide?" He smiled. "So, to continue on this path of exploration, *cariño*, can I interest you in dessert?"

"Of course," Binky said. "What did you have in mind?"

"Nutella on toast. It's sick how good it is. I'll be right back," Tino said. Then he looked at the line that had formed at the truck and corrected himself. "I'll be back as soon as humanly possible."

Suddenly, however, he did something unexpected. Leaning down, he brushed his lips against Binky's. "By the way, you don't need Prada," he said softly. "You'd look gorgeous in a paper sack. Now, I'm going to go get us that dessert."

CHAPTER 11

UNFORTUNATELY, romantic dates aside, there was still a party to plan. And that meant— shopping.

The day after Binky's date, the *amigas* stood outside the Bal Harbour mall slurping down lemonades, waiting for Binky and her crew. They were meeting the *damas* and *chambelanes*, to hold the fittings for their outfits. Even though the *quince*'s court consisted of just seven girls and seven guys, it always felt—at least to the *amigas*—as if they were wrangling a cast of thousands.

Jamie was wearing a black-and-white-striped T-shirt and a cropped black leather jacket. Carmen had on a vintage señorita dress from her mom that she'd dyed bright turquoise. Alicia sported a black halter-top jumpsuit. They were dressed to handle anything, because this was turning out to be their most complicated *quinceañera* yet.

Who knew that if you were going to have 250 people on a yacht you had to have the plumber install a thousand dollars' worth of extra pipes, so that the sensitive bathrooms wouldn't explode? Who knew that the catering trucks could only load at certain docks, because of refrigeration and electrical issues? Who knew that if you were going to take dozens of minors out on the open sea, you needed eight different loading documents, all of which had to be signed by the Miami boating commissioner?

After the last week and a half, the *amigas* knew more about party-planning, yachts, and city government than they had ever thought they would. They kept their clipboards at the ready and went over their checklists with a fine-tooth comb. They were prepared for anything.

Or so they thought.

When the white Cadillac Escalade pulled up and they heard a familiar voice call out, "Wassup, *chicas*?" they were more than a little stunned. Only Binky would show up in a brand-new $80,000 car—just to go shopping for dresses for her *damas*.

"We really shouldn't be surprised," Alicia mused.

"No, we shouldn't," Carmen said.

"And yet, we are," Jamie declared.

Binky got out of the car, as bright as sunshine in a

lemon yellow silk dress and a long navy blue boyfriend cardigan, followed by six other girls.

"Hey, *amigas*, meet my peeps," Binky said. "These are my Everglades Academy girls—Isabella, Carla, Olivia, Brittany, and Blake."

The girls were all dressed in nearly identical silk racer-back T-shirts, skinny jeans, and boyfriend cardigans.

There were hellos, what's-ups, and nods all around.

"And this is Zoe, my best friend from tennis camp," Binky said, giving the girl standing to her left a tight squeeze.

Zoe was petite, Asian American, and dressed from head to toe in Chanel.

"This is my first *quinceañera*, and I'm so excited," she said in a supersugary voice. "I can't wait to tell my friends in Boca all about it."

"Um, Binky, one small problem—I see only six girls, and you should have seven *damas*," Alicia pointed out.

Binky quickly explained that her cousin Lily hadn't been able to make it, but that she was hoping that Carmen—who looked to be about Lily's size—would be willing to try on a dress for her.

The introductions completed, Jamie whispered to Binky, "A Cadillac limo? Was that necessary?"

Binky smiled. "Not necessary, but really fun. Look inside!"

They climbed into the Escalade. The interior was covered from floor to ceiling in leopard-print plush, and there were two flat-screen TVs, leather seats, and a bar.

"This is *nuts*," Jamie said, climbing back out.

"Wait till you see the ones the boys are coming in," Binky said.

Moments later, a black Escalade pulled up in front of the mall, and seven very happy-looking guys got out: Dash; Troy; Tino; and four others, from the Everglades football team, who, judging from the way they ran over to smooch Binky's friends Isabella, Olivia, Carla, and Brittany, were also those girls' boyfriends.

Jamie hadn't seen Dash since the game, but they'd been texting and talking constantly. Now she felt the familiar butterflies in her stomach as he came to stand next to her. Trying to hide her nerves, she gave him a fake punch in the shoulder. "So, this is how you roll?" she asked.

"You know it's not me; it's Binky," he said, blushing a little.

"Still, it must be fun to have a little sister who's so OTT," Jamie said playfully.

"Oh, yeah," Dash said. "All I have do is golf, keep my

grades up, and go along for the ride."

Jamie reached out for his hand and squeezed it. "I like a guy who's got his priorities straight."

Binky, meanwhile, had quickly made her way over to Tino, who whispered something in her ear. She giggled. Turning to Carmen, she said, "You know, I owe you for introducing me to your brother."

Tino shook his head. "I'm the one who owes her. I would've never met you if she hadn't invited you over to the house."

Despite the cheesiness, Carmen grinned. She and Domingo were probably still like that. "I love that you both feel you owe me. And I wouldn't mind at all if Tino took on more chores for the next, say, six months. Especially since I've got bathroom duty this week and dishes for the foreseeable future. But the important thing, lovebirds, is to be good to *each other*."

Carmen looked at her brother and Binky, then over at Dash and Jamie. Was it really true that opposites attracted? Or maybe it was just that, when given the chance to meet and mingle, people who seemed really different had more in common than it appeared? Whatever the reason, she was glad everyone seemed happy.

Now that both groups were there, it was time to call the meeting to order. Alicia stood on a bench in front of the mall. "Hey, you guys. Listen up. There's a lot to do, and not a lot of time. *Damas*—ladies—I'd like you to go with Binky and Carmen to try on your dresses. *Chambelanes*, come with me and Jamie to try on your outfits. We'll meet back at Zanetti's for lunch at twelve thirty; then it's over to my house—I guess we'll be traveling in these ridunculous limos—for dance rehearsal. Got it?"

Everyone nodded in agreement and, following orders, split up into teams of girls and boys.

Carmen had reserved the bridal-party dressing room at Neiman Marcus, and, chatting and giggling, they quickly made their way there.

"Are you the Mortimer wedding party?" the older woman at the front desk asked when they arrived. The girls began to giggle even louder.

Carmen shook her head. "No actually, it's the Mortimer *quinceañera*. It's as big as a wedding. . . ."

"But I get to stay single!" Binky yelled.

"Woo-hoo!" Binky's girls screamed in agreement.

The saleswoman was completely unfazed. "My apologies, it shouldn't be a problem. Believe me, we get a lot of *quinceañeras* here."

She led them behind an emerald green velvet curtain

and into a huge dressing room with hardwood ebony floors dotted with ivory plush chaise longues and banquettes. Each seating area was covered in either a white or camel cashmere throw. Giant mirrors in ornate silver frames were propped up against every wall.

"I've died and gone to shopping heaven," Binky said, plopping down on a chaise longue. "You can come and get me in two weeks."

"You and me both," Carmen said, jumping into a high-backed tufted chair that came startlingly close to being a throne. "I love creating my original designs. But you know, shopping is nice, too."

There was a collective squeal from the party as four salesgirls in identical black dresses wheeled in the two racks of dresses that Carmen had preordered. And the waiters who arrived with silver trays of Voss water and ice also received the stamp of approval of Binky and her posse.

So far, so good, Carmen thought.

Then the dresses were tried on—and the drama began.

Binky's *quince* gown was a brilliant tangerine color, and it had been Carmen's idea that the *damas* would all wear navy, to add a nautical touch to the Princess of the Tides theme.

Reality, however, quickly came crashing in when Isabella announced that she only wore purple, since that was her signature color. Brittany followed suit, saying she simply could not be seen at what was surely going to be the party of the year in anything other than Tiffany blue, since that was *her* signature color. Carla felt that navy overwhelmed her fair complexion, and Olivia, who had dark skin, felt as if she needed a color that would really pop. Blake was fine with navy but didn't want to wear a floor-length dress, since her legs, as she explained, were her best feature. And Zoe took off for Chanel, because off-the-rack shopping depressed her.

Two hours later, nothing had been decided. The girls had moved on from Voss to Diet Cokes and were beginning to bounce off the walls from all the caffeine. The sales staff brought out freshly baked Neiman Marcus chocolate-chip cookies made from a secret recipe, and Binky and her friends, completely side-tracked from the task at hand, began trying on Christian Louboutin espadrilles (needless to say, the espadrilles, while very cute, were of absolutely no relevance to Binky's *quince*).

When her cell phone rang an hour later, Carmen, who was not an easy girl to fluster, ducked inside a changing room and burst into tears.

"Hello," she sputtered.

"Yo, what's wrong?" Jamie asked, on the other end of the line.

"Binky's *damas* won't wear anything I present to them," Carmen said through her tears. "They are completely and totally out of control, and Binky is no help. She just keeps saying, 'Cool with me. Cool with me.' Well, you know what? I'm in charge of the fashion for this *quinceañera*, and when Binky gets the pictures of her big day, I'm the one she'll yell at because her girls look like party-girl jesters and not proper *damas* in a *quince* court."

Jamie sighed. "Do you need me to step in and get a little Bronx over there?"

"I think I do," Carmen sniffed. "But aren't you busy with the *chambelanes*?"

"*Amiga*, please," Jamie said. "Those guys did exactly what we told them to do. We were done in half an hour. Alicia and I went and got our nails done."

Carmen couldn't believe it. "All this time, you've been getting a manicure?"

"Yeah, I got this supercute dark burgundy color. It's called Wicked," Jamie said. Carmen let out a growl.

Jamie knew not to push the issue. "I've got three

minutes under this dryer; then I'm on my way over to you."

As promised, Jamie showed up shortly afterward at the lounge of the disobedient *damas,* who had gone from trying on Louboutins to checking out Uggs.

"Okay, listen up, because I'm only going to say this once," Jamie announced to the small crowd of girls. "This is Binky's *quince,* not your *quince.* I don't want to hear any more mess about your signature colors. I could care less about your likes and dislikes, best features and worst features. You've got one job as members of Binky's court, and that is to be a pal to Binky, who has decided to take part in this pretty awesome Latina rite of passage. You should be *honored* that she's asked you to be part of it. You should be *thrilled* that you are getting a free dress. You should be *over the moon* that in a month from now, you'll be on a yacht, shaking your groove thing at the most amazing *quince* the greater Miami area has ever seen. Do you understand me?"

All of the girls nodded. Zoe, who had slipped back into the lounge in the middle of Jamie's speech, added an enthusiastic "Woo-hoo!"

"Now, when I count to three, I want you all to say, 'Thank you, Binky, Birthday Girl!' One . . . two . . . three!"

"Thank you, Binky, Birthday Girl!" they all cried in unison.

Jamie smiled. "Nicely done. Now, I want you all to come over to me, and all I want to hear is one word, or number, rather: your size—two, four, six, eight, ten, or twelve. My associate will hand you a dress, and then we are outta here."

And just like that, order returned. In less than fifteen minutes, all of the *damas'* dresses had been purchased. Even more surprisingly, everyone seemed genuinely happy.

Unfortunately, later that afternoon, back at Alicia's, the *amigas* discovered that the shopping for Binky's *damas* and *chambelanes* had been a walk in the park compared to teaching them how to dance.

Binky had her heart set on a traditional Latin ballroom number for the presentation of her court. But while all of her girls could walk in heels, none of them— including Binky—could dance in them.

Alicia kept pausing the rumba number that she and Binky had selected, but no matter how many times they practiced the steps, the only ones who could do any of the moves were Jamie (standing in for Binky's cousin), Dash, and Tino.

Finally, after four hours of trying, an exhausted Binky asked, "Isn't it possible for my dad to take the mike and just introduce the court? And no dancing?"

"Hmmm." Alicia looked out into the distance.

"What does 'hmmm' mean?" Binky asked Jamie.

"'Hmmm' means that we pride ourselves on *quinces* that go above and beyond in every category," Jamie said, translating. "If your dad's going to just emcee all of the big moments, then why hire us?"

Alicia's gaze grew suddenly focused. "I think I have an idea."

And indeed she did.

True, Amigas Inc. prided itself as a group on going the extra mile, but even Alicia knew when to give up. If she couldn't force complicated moves on the court, she'd go back to basics—work with what they *could* do. After quickly figuring out some simplified moves, Alicia got to work crafting a number.

And by the time all of the *damas* and *chambelanes* left, two hours later, they were all gloriously in step.

CHAPTER 12

THE FOLLOWING Wednesday afternoon found Jamie walking up the front steps of the Mortimer mansion. She'd been at the house more than a half a dozen times since the *amigas* had started planning Binky's *quinceañera* and since she had started seeing Dash, but it was still quite a shock to see the ginormous place that Binky and Dash called home. How many rooms had Binky said it had? Twenty-five? Thirty?

She'd also met Dash and Binky's father, Chip, in passing several times over the course of her visits. He seemed like a nice guy, even though she blamed him for the family's apparent preference for odd nicknames. Now she rang the doorbell, feeling herself relax when the family butler opened the door.

"Miss Sosa," Sherwood said, in his singsongy Bermudan accent, "do come in."

She thanked him and explained that she'd come by

to drop off favor samples for Binky. Though her *quince* was rapidly approaching, Binky still hadn't decided on the gifts for her guests. Traditionally, the *damas* and *chambelanes* got personalized presents, and each of the party guests got a simpler, more general gift— like a keychain that said, BINKY'S FIFTEENTH—as a favor. Jamie knew that Binky thought she could wait to decide, because money was not an object. Time, on the other hand, *was* an object.

Mission accomplished—or explanation delivered— Jamie handed Sherwood the bag of gift samples and just was about to leave when she heard a particularly sexy voice call her name. Despite the fact that they had been on several dates by now, kissed countless times, and talked on the phone for dozens of hours (or so it seemed), she still shivered when she heard Dash's voice. And she still found herself amazed that someone like him would be into someone like her—and that *she* could be into *him*.

"Hey," she said, turning around. "I thought you had an interview with *Golf World* magazine."

"The reporter got food poisoning and had to reschedule, so I'm home early," he explained.

He looked as cute as ever in a yellow polo shirt and navy golf shorts.

Jamie kissed him on the cheek. "Well, it's nice to see you," she said, beaming.

"I was just sitting on the patio with my stepmother," Dash said. "I don't think you've met her yet."

"Nope," Jamie said, shaking her head. The stepmother had been suspiciously absent from all Binky's party-planning. As Binky had explained, the stepmonster cared only about one thing—herself. As long as Amigas Inc. made it *look* as though she cared about her stepdaughter, she'd leave them alone.

"You should meet her," he said, taking Jamie's hand. "I promise you, her snarl is much worse than her bite. Most of the time." He laughed, trying to reassure her.

Holding his hand, she followed him onto the patio. Her heart was racing. A bronze woman in a bright, papaya-colored sundress sat motionless, wearing a giant pair of sunglasses.

Dash smiled and said, "Bev, this is my girlfriend, Jamie. Jamie, my stepmom, Bev."

The beating of her heart grew faster—but in a good way. Dash had called her his girlfriend—totally unprompted—in front of a major parental unit. Wow, she thought, mentally pinching herself.

With renewed confidence—after all, she *was* Dash's

official girlfriend—Jamie extended her hand. "Pleased to meet you, Mrs. Mortimer."

Bev limply returned her handshake but said nothing.

Both Binky and Dash had complained about their stepmother and how her only interests were money and other people with money. Still, even though she'd been forewarned, Jamie felt a little wounded by what was obviously a brush-off.

She was just formulating a plan of escape when Dash ruined it. "I have a great idea, Jamie. Why don't you join us for a family dinner Saturday night?"

Mrs. Mortimer evidently liked the idea about as much as Jamie did. "Oh, but, Dash, dear, we're having dinner at the club that night."

He shrugged. "And . . . ?"

Mrs. Mortimer pushed the glasses down on her nose and gave Jamie a once-over. "There's a dress code."

"And . . . ?" Dash repeated.

"That means no tennis shoes. No hip-hop gear. Nothing so *urban* as what she's wearing right now, dear."

Jamie willed herself not to let her Bronx slip out. "No problem," she said, through gritted teeth. Suddenly, she felt as if she were thirteen again and the token minority member at an unwelcoming boarding school.

"You can always join us another night," Bev went on, finally addressing her directly. "We tend to be much more relaxed at home."

Jamie shook her head. "I'm perfectly comfortable with coming to dinner at the club. I went to Fitzgibbons Academy, you know."

Both Dash and his stepmother looked surprised at this revelation. Mrs. Mortimer took her sunglasses completely off and stared at Jamie a little more attentively.

"Fitzgibbons is a very good school," she said. "And where do you go now?"

Jamie squared her shoulders, determined not to let Bev Mortimer get the best of her.

"I go to Coral Gables High School," she replied.

Mrs. Mortimer put her sunglasses back on. "Public school?" She practically sneered the words. "Pity."

Dash didn't bother to hide his anger. "We'll be leaving now, Bev. Have a good rest of the afternoon."

Jamie knew she should have said, "Nice to meet you, Mrs. Mortimer," but she just couldn't. Instead, she simply followed Dash back inside the house.

At the front door, Dash said, "I'd love to give you a ride. Make up for my stepmother's utter lack of manners. I'm sorry she was like that. I hope it didn't upset you."

"Forget about it," Jamie said, struggling to keep her composure in front of him. "Trust me, if you didn't live on this crazy island, I'd take you up on the offer. But you'd have to take the ferry to your car, then drive to my house and back again. It's a sweet offer, and I appreciate it, but I could really use some time alone to think."

After a few more attempts to persuade her, Dash agreed to let her go home alone. But not without first giving her a sweet, long kiss good-bye.

Jamie fumed the whole way home. She kept replaying the conversation in her head, kept seeing the way Bev had dismissed her with one glance, the way the corners of her mouth had turned down in a frown when she said "public school."

The moment Jamie got home, she went straight to the garage. At that point, she wondered if she weren't more angry than hurt. All she knew was that the complex web of emotions rolling around inside her was causing her a lot of pain, and it was time to pump up Badly Drawn Boy. One of her British suitemates at Fitzgibbons had played the band's music all the time. Jamie hated the band at first, but eventually it had grown on her. Whenever she felt like painting her heart out, BDB was the perfect music—melodic, tortured, primal.

She must really have cranked it, because a few minutes later, her mother came out.

"Whoa, no future plans for your eardrums, huh?" her mother said.

Jamie turned the music down.

"What's wrong?" her mother asked. "Is it the *quince*?"

Jamie shook her head.

"Is it Dash? I thought things were going really well with you two."

"They are," Jamie said miserably.

"Then what's the problem, *hija*?" Zulema asked, making herself comfortable on the studio couch.

"Dash invited me to a family dinner at the country club, and his snooty stepmother kept going on about the dress code and country-club standards like I was someone who had no class at all," Jamie explained.

Her mother got up, smiling, and came over to her daughter. "I, for one, love it when people underestimate me," she said, resting a gentle hand on her shoulder. "You'll put on a nice dress, you'll go to dinner, and you'll knock their socks off, because you are one impressive young woman."

"Why should I want to impress her?" Jamie asked.

"Be the bigger person, *hija*."

"*Why* should I be the bigger person? Because she's

rich and I'm not?" Jamie asked, exasperated.

"You should be the bigger person," her mother said softly, "because you are the incredible Jamie Sosa. And she's not."

With that, her mother kissed her on the forehead and left the studio. Jamie was once again alone with just her thoughts for company.

Every time her mind drifted to the idea of dinner at the club, all she could think of was the pinched, distasteful expression on Bev Mortimer's face. The look that said, *You don't belong here. You don't belong with a guy like Dash.*

Jamie wanted to believe that she was being too sensitive. Her mother always said, "What people think of you is none of your business." But at Fitzgibbons, Jamie had encountered plenty of Bev Mortimers and their daughters, and it had left a nasty taste in her mouth. As much as she didn't want to think back to those days, the memories suddenly rushed back, impossible to suppress.

There had been her art teacher, Mrs. Ward, who had accused Jamie of plagiarizing her term paper, "Picasso, the Ultimate Player." Mrs. Ward had been so convinced that Jamie could not have written such a sophisticated analysis of the relationship between the artist's work and his affairs with women that she'd taken the case all the way to the dean, in the hopes of having Jamie expelled. It was only when Jamie agreed to submit to an oral exam on Picasso's life and work with the entire art department that the plagiarism charges had been dropped.

Even now, just thinking about the whole incident made her furious. It had been utterly unfair. Her parents might not have gone to fancy colleges, but they'd seen a little bit of the world. *Guernica* had been her father's favorite painting ever since he was a high school student and saw a play that used the Spanish Civil War and Picasso's iconic painting as a metaphor for the sugarcane wars between Haiti and the Dominican Republic. And her mother might not have been able to afford a real Picasso, but she had poster reproductions of his work that she cherished.

As for her own theories about Picasso's psychology as a cheating dog with majorly ambivalent feelings toward women, all Jamie had had to do was read Françoise Gilot's memoir. Gilot was the only woman who had had the strength to leave him.

It wasn't rocket science, Jamie remembered thinking. I just did my research.

Being called a cheat had hurt her. And while she had had her fair share of run-ins with social ostracism at the hands of mean girls, her position as the freak of the school hadn't been complete until she started hanging out with Nils Stotter.

Jamie'd had no interest in Nils, the son of a Swedish ambassador, when she first met him. But never having gotten close to the girls in her dorm, she was happy for the company he seemed willing to provide. She had liked to tease him for his fondness for wearing knee-length shorts and dark socks. He'd called it the Bermudan business suit, but Jamie had let him know that he was firmly in *Sound of Music* territory.

Once they'd started hanging out, they soon fell into a pattern. Every Friday night they went to see a film at the student center. Afterward, Nils would walk her back to her dorm. One night, he asked her, very formally, "May I hold your hand?" She had nodded, more surprised than excited. But when her hand was in his, Jamie had marveled at how long and smooth his fingers were and how warm his hand was as he grasped hers on the cool Connecticut evening. It was as if he had had a warm ball of coal sewn into his palms, transmitting heat from his hand to hers.

For weeks, Jamie had let herself bask in the warmth of Nils's attention. He walked her to class, sat with her in the lunchroom, joined her at assembly. On Sunday afternoons, Nils cooked her traditional Scandinavian meals from ingredients that his grandmother shipped over in big wooden crates: Swedish meatballs, mashed potatoes with lingonberries, salmon gravlax with mustard sauce. She was still a girl who loved her *lechón*, her rice, and her beans, but Nils got her to fall for new foods, and, in the process, she fell for him, too. Hard.

Then Parents' Weekend had arrived. On that Saturday morning, all of the parents had gathered in the great hall of the big stone building that had been the original residence. Adults milled around, holding cups of coffee and agendas. Nils, Jamie, and the other students were dressed in their charcoal gray blazers, the boys in red and gold ties, the girls in red and gold pleated skirts.

Her own parents couldn't make it, so Jamie had volunteered to work at the event for a little spending money. She was sitting at the information table, greeting new parents and giving them their necessary information, when Nils walked over with his parents and introduced her to them.

Nils's mother had thin blond hair, pale pink lips, and high cheekbones, like an art-house movie star. She was perfectly lovely to Jamie, asking questions about the Bronx and Jamie's artwork that made it clear that Nils had spoken of her a lot.

And then—"Papa, this is my friend Jamie," Nils had said. But Nils's father had looked right through Jamie in a way that made her feel two clicks past awful. Just like that, her good mood had vanished.

Ambassador Stotter continued to ignore Jamie and spoke only to Nils. "Where is the dean, son? Does she know that I'm here?"

Nils spoke again, firmly this time. "Papa. Please say hello to my friend Jamie."

His father kept his eyes focused on the wall directly above Jamie's head. "Nils," Ambassador Stotter said, "I'm only here for one day. Let's prioritize."

Then he strode away. She had never learned what happened in those few hours between the time Nils turned to follow his father and the next morning, when she saw him at breakfast. But whatever it was, it changed everything.

"Hey, where are you sitting?" Jamie said when he walked in with his mother that morning. "I'll join you."

Nils shook his head and wouldn't meet her eyes. "I'm having breakfast alone with my mom, if that's okay."

After Parents' Weekend was over, Nils went back to having lunch with the embassy kids—the sons and daughters of diplomats, who at various points had known one another at the United Nations International

School in New York. He never spoke to her again. And she didn't have the strength or courage to confront him and ask him what the hell was up.

Shaking her head, Jamie refocused. Enough of the painful past, she thought. She had to work. She had been doing a Warhol-style portrait of Binky as a birthday present from Amigas Inc. and began to fill in one of the quadrants, then thought better of it. She was too mad to paint, and paint was too expensive to waste.

Her cell phone rang, and she looked at the number. Dash.

"Are you still upset?" he asked when she answered.

"No," she said, lying.

"Well, I would be if I were you," he said. "But the secret to dealing with Bev is to not let her manipulate you. If you don't come Saturday, it's like she told you to stay away and you did."

Jamie was silent. In one short conversation with Bev Mortimer, all her insecurities had come rushing back, and Jamie wasn't sure whom she was madder at—Bev, for being so condescending—or herself, for letting it get to her.

"You there?" Dash asked when the silence had dragged on for several moments.

"I'm here."

"Please come to dinner," Dash pleaded. "It would mean a lot to me to have you there."

Jamie thrust her shoulders back. "I'll be there," she said.

And she silently added, *in my own fashion.*

CHAPTER 13

EVERYTHING ABOUT the West Side Country Club was designed to intimidate—at least, that was the way it felt to Jamie. Approaching the main building, she had a flashback to the time when she was eight years old and watched *The Wizard of Oz* on TV for the first time. The perfectly manicured driveway reminded her of the yellow brick road, and the magnificent building that was set high on the hill looked just like the palatial dwelling that Dorothy and Toto visited in the Emerald City.

The Mortimers were already at the club when Jamie arrived. Dash and his father had met for their usual Saturday round of golf. Dash had been beating his father at the game since he was nine years old, but they both cherished the time they spent together, even if the likelihood of any real competition was slim.

While the boys played golf, the women spent the

day at the spa. Bev had what was called a medical facial and what Binky referred to as a professional spackle and grout. Binky got a manicure, pedicure, and blowout. She had invited Jamie to join them, but Jamie had passed. She needed time to prepare. She'd decided to make a statement at dinner, to let Bev Mortimer know exactly what she thought of her stupid club with its stupid dress code and rules.

So she had dressed in an old-school Wild Style T-shirt and a Day-Glo pink spandex miniskirt over supertight skinny jeans. On her feet were a pair of canary yellow Converse high-heeled sneakers. On one arm, she wore a gaggle of studded black-leather bracelets; on the other arm, she'd carefully painted an intricately designed fake tattoo. She knew it was a bit much, but rightly or wrongly, she felt impelled to run the risk of ruining everything to make her point. To that end, she'd gone completely extreme with her makeup—tons of black eyeliner, black mascara, and bold red lipstick.

She topped the whole ensemble with a classic Burberry trench that she'd scored for just ten dollars at her favorite consignment store. The lining and hem had been in tatters, but Carmen had hooked it up with a purple-check trim that made it look not merely as good as new, but positively haute couture.

When Ferris, the Mortimers' driver, showed up at Jamie's house to get her, he'd tried to persuade her to change.

"Miss Sosa, far be it from me to question your sartorial choices," he said, "but I do believe there's a dress code at the club."

Jamie feigned ignorance and tugged at her trench coat. "Is Burberry banned, Ferris?" she asked.

"No, ma'am, the trench coat is quite fetching," he said. "I'm referring to your jeans and sneakers."

Jamie smiled brightly. "Oh, the jeans and sneakers are quite on purpose," she said. Then, looking at her watch, she added, "We'd better go, Ferris. I'd hate to be late for dinner."

Ferris coughed. "I'm sure that I could call ahead to Dash and explain that we'll just be a few more minutes."

Jamie wouldn't be swayed. "No need! I'm ready to go."

But now, as she sat in the back of the silver Bentley, Jamie felt her courage waning. Her actions were going to have repercussions, there was no doubt about that. And for the first time, she realized that those actions would have impact not only on her. Binky was a client. Her parents were paying for this outing.

Jamie shuddered. What was done was done. She could only hope that Mr. Mortimer didn't fire her on the spot and that Dash and Binky would understand that she wasn't trying to be disrespectful, she was just trying to teach their stepmother that stereotypes were ridiculous. If Bev Mortimer wanted to treat her like some extreme conception of a girl from the hood, then Jamie was going to show up and represent the hood, to the max.

All too soon, they arrived. Ferris parked the car and escorted her to the opulent dining room. The domed ceiling must've been thirty feet high, and globes made of tiny gold lights hung down like planets in the solar system.

Each table was covered with an ivory tablecloth, and the plates were hand-painted with gold stars and accents. A classical music trio played softly on a raised stage, and Jamie was surprised at how lovely she found the whole scene. Once, during her time at Fitzgibbons Academy, one of her suitemates' parents had taken all the girls in their suite to dinner at Tavern on the Green. Despite how generally miserable she'd been at Fitzgibbons, she'd had a nice time that night. Everything had seemed special and memorable—from the fairy lights twinkling in the trees to the horse-drawn carriage ride through Central Park to which the girls had been treated after dinner.

For a moment, Jamie considered turning around, going home to change, and coming back another night, when she and Dash could have a fancy grown-up dinner without his frosty stepmother around. But this wasn't just about her, Jamie reminded herself. It was about standing up for all Latinas—letting Bev Mortimer know that not every Hispanic with brown skin and dark hair was a *chola* from East L.A.

She took off her trench coat and revealed her ensemble. She could feel diners at the nearest tables turn and stare. She stared back, defiantly.

Ferris spoke to the maître d'. "This is Miss Sosa, with the Mortimer party."

"Miss Sosa," said the maître d', looking down his ski-slope nose. "I'll be happy to seat you momentarily. But it would seem the Mortimers did not explain that there is a dress code for the dining room. T-shirts are frowned upon. Jeans and sneakers are not permitted under any circumstances."

Jamie looked around, emboldened by the attention she was receiving. "That's ridiculous!" she said loudly. "As you can see, I'm wearing a skirt over jeans, and the sneakers not only have heels, they're limited editions."

The maître d' cleared his throat and lowered his voice, as if to neutralize her loud tone. "Miss Sosa, if you would permit me, we keep spare clothes and shoes on hand for occasions such as this. I can assure you that they are perfectly appropriate."

Jamie shook her head. "And I can assure you that my best friend's father is deputy mayor, and I can have this whole place closed for discriminatory practices."

The maître d' looked horrified. Jamie smirked. All those hours of watching *Law and Order* were finally coming in handy.

She heard a cough behind her and turned around to find Dash and his father standing there. Dash looked confused. Mr. Mortimer looked bemused. "I hope an exception can be made for our guest," he said calmly, his silver hair and dark gray suit epitomizing class.

"Of course, sir," the maître d' said. "May we ask that the young lady keep the trench coat on?"

"I've got no problem with that," Jamie said with a nod, "as long as I get to keep my sneakers on. You never know when I'll have to dine and dash." She laughed and pointed to Dash. "Get it? Dine and *Dash!*"

Her boyfriend did not look amused. "What the hell are you up to?" he hissed in her ear, as he guided her firmly into the dining room.

As she followed him, she whispered, "Just keeping it real D., just keeping it real."

When they arrived at the table, Bev Mortimer was waiting. She still wore her sunglasses and only barely turned to acknowledge Jamie's presence.

Binky got up and, of course, gave Jamie a big hug. "Hey, *amiga*, what's up?"

"Really, Binky," Bev said, finally deigning to speak. "Must you be so ethnic in your displays of affection?"

All of a sudden, Jamie understood why Binky was such a big hugger. It drove her stepmother batty. It was also clear that Jamie's getup was working Bev Mortimer's last nerve. Behind her glasses, Binky's step-mother vacillated between scanning the room and staring at Jamie. Finally, she spoke to their guest.

"Would you really have us believe that you have no suitable clothes for a dinner out?" she asked. "Even the dress you had on yesterday was an improvement over this ensemble."

Jamie, who had begun to feel slightly silly, turned indignant again. "Funny, I think that most people would agree that my outfit is much more stylish than yours."

Mrs. Mortimer was about to respond when the waiter came by with their first course. "To start your meal, we're serving a lobster salad with sunchoke mayonnaise and pickled tomato," he said.

Jamie picked up a fork.

"The smaller one, dear," Bev said with a smirk.

And that was when it hit Jamie.

Her plan had backfired. The joke was on her. Jamie *knew* her salad fork from her dinner fork. She and Amigas Inc. had set hundreds of tables for *quinceañera* celebrations, and Jamie had always taken great pleasure in getting every detail perfect.

But Bev Mortimer had made her so mad that she'd not only forgotten her basic table manners, she'd forgotten who she really was. She was proud of her Bronx pedigree, proud to rep the boogie-down as Jamie from the block. But part of that girl's identity was as a girl who'd spent hours at the Cloisters staring at the Unicorn tapestries. A girl who spent hours on eBay looking for gorgeous vintage dresses. A girl who loved beautiful things and beautiful evenings just like this one. Being really mad at Bev Mortimer had made her behave in a way that did nothing to highlight the *belleza* of her Latina spirit. She'd embarrassed herself, her people . . . and Amigas Inc.

Despite the fact that she was starving and that the one bite of lobster salad she had had was the most delicious thing she'd eaten in a long time, Jamie pushed her plate away. "Thank you for inviting me to dinner. But I should be going." She stood up.

"I'll come with you," Dash said, but his voice was stiff.

"No, please. Stay," she said. "I need some time alone."

"Fine," Dash said, exasperated. "Apparently, you're tough enough to take care of yourself."

Jamie willed herself not to cry as she walked back through the elaborate dining room. She looked straight ahead, shoulders back, head held high—the confident walk her *mami* had taught her when she was just a little girl. But she could feel that everyone's eyes were on her, and this time, it wasn't a good feeling.

As soon as she was safely outside, Jamie texted Gaz to come get her. He was the only person she knew who wouldn't judge her—she hoped. She couldn't stand the idea of telling her *chicas* what she had just done. They wouldn't have believed it—and they'd probably have been pissed. She had put their jobs in jeopardy. For all she knew, they might not even have jobs after her little display.

In less than twenty minutes, Gaz pulled up at the front door of the club, in his beat-up old sedan.

"So, *chica*, I guess you're not planning on becoming

a member of the Mortimers' country club any time soon," Gaz said when she got in on the passenger side. "Was it really as bad as you said in your text?"

Jamie nodded.

"Do you want to talk about it?" he asked. Jamie shook her head.

"Okay," he said gently. "Then I'll leave you alone. I'm here when you're ready."

Jamie flipped open her phone. She was hoping there'd be a message from Dash, although she had no idea what she expected it to say. Maybe: *Thanks for embarrassing me in front of my parents and my country club friends.* Or maybe it would read: *U R so cute in yr skinny jeans!* Or perhaps Jamie had underestimated her role as a trendsetter, and Dash was texting to say: *Some of the ladies at the club were hoping you'd hook them up with your stylist.*

Mostly, she hoped for a text that said: *Wait for me. I'll come with you.*

But there was no such text. She'd been staring at her phone so intently that she didn't notice that Gaz hadn't left the country club parking lot.

"Are you ready to go?" Gaz asked.

"I guess so," she said.

He put the car into gear and drove down the long

driveway. "You didn't stay long enough to eat anything, I bet," he said. "You must be hungry."

Jamie wanted to hug him. He was not pushing. Not bothering her. He was just letting her be. "Starving like Marvin," she said quietly.

Gaz nodded. "There's a Pollo Loco on Collins Avenue, before we hit the ninety-five," he said. "Wanna drive through?"

Jamie smiled genuinely for the first time all evening. "I would *love* that."

Driving through the Pollo Loco reminded Jamie of all the times she had gone there with Carmen and Alicia. She felt a sudden urge to text the girls immediately. Then she remembered that she'd have had to explain why she wasn't dining on seared arctic char with Dash and his family. And that she might have just blown their biggest job ever. Maybe texting them wasn't a good idea. She sank back against the car's worn leather seats and ate her arroz con pollo in silence.

Jamie didn't sleep very well that night. Her mind was racing. She had talked things over with Gaz, but she still felt a huge weight of guilt despite his assurances that she could fix things—probably.

The next day, she thought about calling Dash or

sending him an e-mail. She looked across the bedroom and saw the vase full of the last of Dash's very resilient roses. She had a better idea.

She took out the debit card for her savings account and put it in her purse. After a quick shower, she threw on a hoodie and jeans and took the bus to Elsa's Jardin, the florist that Amigas recommended to all its clients.

The girls loved the bright, airy shop, with its garage-style back and front doors. There was a café in the middle of the shop where they had spent many hours sipping lattes, going over flower orders for their clients, feeling absolutely and positively grown-up.

Now she was there on a different sort of business. Walking into the giant fridge, Jamie pulled out a bouquet of purple hydrangeas and a bunch of pink hibiscus. She brought them to the counter and watched as Elly, the manager, wrapped the flowers in brown butcher paper and the pink and green tartan ribbon that Jamie had picked out.

Finally, she wrote a brief note of apology to the Mortimers and attached it to the pink hibiscus. And then she wrote a note to Dash. She used the same words he had used when he'd sent flowers to her: *"Discúlpame, discúlpame, discúlpame, discúlpame, discúlpame—forgive me, forgive me, forgive me—Jamie."*

CHAPTER 14

JAMIE DIDN'T HEAR anything from Dash that day, and she became more and more despondent. She imagined him receiving the flowers and frowning. Throwing them in the trash and wiping his hands. She worried that he'd perhaps never received her flowers at all. Then she imagined he had but that the whole family had gathered around her pitiful excuse of a note and laughed at her. By the end of the day, she was a wreck.

But early the next morning, before school, she came downstairs and found a surprise. Dash was sitting at the kitchen table, having breakfast with her father.

"*Hola, querida,*" Mr. Sosa said, lifting his cup of coffee.

"*Hola, querida,*" Dash repeated.

She was wearing a vintage camisole and a pair of old pajama pants and felt embarrassed. "Um, excuse me, I'm just going to grab a robe," she said.

When she returned, Dash was still at the table, and her father was putting his dishes in the sink. "I've got to go to work, and your mother is at the grocery store. But I think I can trust the two of you alone in the house."

"Of course, *Papi*," she said, kissing him on the cheek.

He left, and Jamie poured herself a glass of orange juice. She sat down next to Dash. It was puzzling to see him in her house, especially when he'd never responded to her flowers.

"I don't mean to be rude, but what are you doing here?" Jamie asked. Even at seven o'clock in the morning, he looked deliciously handsome.

Dash smiled. "Well, my family and I got your flowers and your notes. All is forgiven. True, your note to me was not the most original in the world. But it was effective. And probably more effective because you thought to include the rest of the family. Bev is a sucker for pretty flowers. And really, when it comes down to it, you left before you did irreparable damage." He winked to show her he was teasing about the damage part.

As the news of her pardon sank in, Jamie spread some jam on a piece of toast and helped herself to a few pieces of bacon from the plate in the center of the table.

"Why didn't you call?" she finally asked.

Dash poured himself a cup of coffee. "I spent a lot

of time last night thinking about what you said when we first met. I kept thinking, are we just so different that this will never work? And I was worried that maybe it wouldn't.

"Then I thought about all the games of golf I've played," he went on. "All the impossible shots. The whiffs. The water hazards. So many of those shots they said I could never make only *looked* hard. They weren't that difficult once I could tune out all the noise. And that's what I came here this morning to tell you, Jamie. I didn't want to text you. I didn't want to call you. I wanted to tell you in person that this—meaning you and me—is going to work. It's not as hard as it looks if we can just tune out all the noise."

Jamie didn't know what to say. She was so overcome with emotion that when she took a swig of orange juice it went down the wrong way. She began to choke, and Dash had to jump up and pat her on the back.

"Are you okay?" he asked, sounding worried.

"I am," she said, when she'd finally recovered. "More than okay. I think I'm falling in love with you."

"Well, you're a little late to the party, because I fell in love with you the moment I saw you," Dash said.

He leaned forward to kiss her.

"Wait!" she cried and ran out of the room.

Five minutes later she returned.

"I'm ready for that kiss now," she said, putting her hand on her hip saucily.

"Where'd you go?" he asked, puzzled.

"I had to brush my teeth!" she said. "If you're going to show up at a *chica*'s house at the crack of dawn, the least you could do is give her a little notice."

Then she moved closer and kissed him, again and again.

A few days later, still glowing from her talk with Dash, Jamie met Carmen, Alicia, and Binky for a walk-through with the caterers, Fete a Fales. She wanted to tell the girls everything that had happened, but things had been so busy with school and planning that there had never been a good time. Plus, she knew that her first priority had to be the job—especially after her near miss at the country club on Sunday.

Fete was the best in Miami and had catered everything from movie premieres to state dinners. Their office was a modern three-story house in a swanky part of town. Having been there before, the girls knew the way. They entered through the garage and took the stairs up to the second floor, which held a giant loft kitchen, a dining area for tastings, and the company office.

Tilda Fales, the owner of the catering company, was British and in her mid-thirties. She had red hair, freckles, and a cool Notting Hill style. On this particular day, she was wearing skinny jeans, a pale gray cashmere turtleneck, Bromley boots, and an Alexander McQueen capelet. Flawless style aside, she made the most exquisite food, everything from mini Moroccan chicken pot pies to a Peruvian ceviche that was last-supper-worthy.

Tilda greeted the girls and said, *"Feliz cumpleaños"* to Binky. Then they sat down at the long white wooden table next to the floor-to-ceiling glass windows to begin the tastings.

"First up," Tilda said, passing around a purple Lucite tray, "appetizers. We've got mini Reuben sandwiches, Cuban Monte Cristos with mustard and chives, and mascarpone-and-fig bouquets."

"Yum," Alicia said, helping herself to two Monte Cristos.

"The mascarpone-and-fig bouquets are so beautiful," Carmen said admiringly.

"Thanks," Tilda said. "That's our vegetarian option. What do you think, Binky?"

All eyes turned to the *quince*. She, in turn, was looking at the appetizer indifferently. "It's acceptable."

Tilda was understandably perplexed. *Acceptable* was

a word that was *never* associated with the food at a Fete a Fales event.

"Well, if there's anything I can do to make improvements, please let me know," Tilda said. "We want your *quinceañera* to be perfect."

Binky smiled tightly. "Perfect? Like that's going to happen."

Alicia, Carmen, and Jamie exchanged worried glances. This attitude was completely out of character. Jamie had a momentary feeling of panic that her behavior at the dinner was causing this. But then reality hit her. This had nothing to do with dinner.

Binky had become a *quince*-zilla.

Even the nicest girl has her *quince*-zilla freak-out. For some girls, it lasts just a moment; for others, it spans the entire time leading up to their big day. Regardless of the time frame, during this temporary loss of sanity, the *quince* becomes convinced, despite all evidence to the contrary, that everything is going wrong and her *quince* is going to be a complete disaster.

Now it was Binky's turn.

She held up a plate. "Please tell me these aren't the plates we'll be using."

Tilda, who'd seen her share of *quince*-zillas, bridezillas and all other forms of high-maintenance customers, took a deep breath. "You signed off on those plates a week ago."

Binky smiled, making only a minimal effort to hide her annoyance. "You must be mistaken, Tilda," she said. "I would never sign off on *cafeteria white* plates for the most important day of my life! These plates do *not* say, 'Go big or go home!'" Her face was flushed, and she was shaking.

The *amigas* sprang into action.

"Let's take a walk," Carmen said, grabbing Binky by the arm and escorting her down the back stairs towards the office's Japanese rock garden.

"We'll be right back," Alicia said, giving the caterer a reassuring pat on the shoulder.

"We've got this completely under control," Jamie added. "Just give us ten minutes."

"I have the utmost faith in your ability to handle this *petite* crisis," Tilda said, popping a mini Reuben into her mouth. "I'll be in my office when you're ready for me."

The four girls walked out of the building and into the courtyard. Tilda had once explained to them that although Miami's weather would have supported an elaborate, tropical garden, she'd opted to go for the Zen appeal of a Japanese rock garden, because the relationship between a caterer and a client was so often tense. Just standing in the perfectly ordered garden with its soft, smooth stones raked in a way that suggested the rippling of an ocean wave, the *amigas* could feel themselves calming down. Unfortunately, it seemed as though it was going to take a little while longer for the garden to have a similar effect on Binky.

"I can't work with someone who doesn't give me the opportunity to approve the China choices," Binky fumed. "I would never've signed off on those plates."

Carmen spoke first, leading the girls to the low bamboo benches near a row of bright green bushes. "But, *chica*, we signed off on plates days ago."

"*You* did; *I* didn't," Binky said. "Ever since we decided to have the *quince* on our family yacht, I've been planning on having Kate Spade Gwinnett Lane china. The blue and orange match my theme perfectly."

Alicia sighed. "Okay, we'll look into the Kate Spade china. Are we good to return to the tasting?"

Binky shook her head. "I also need to add some names to the guest list."

"Two weeks before the event?" Alicia tried not to sound panicked. The manifest, which had to be signed by the boating commissioner—who, by the way, was not the easiest person to reach—made it clear that the yacht was pushing capacity with a guest-and-crew list that totaled nearly 270. If Binky insisted on more invites, they would probably have to rent a bigger boat. Mr. Mortimer would pay, but Alicia could not even begin to imagine realigning the specs for the current party in a new space, much less one that had to be seaworthy.

"How am I supposed to confine the most important day of my life to two hundred and fifty guests?" Binky wailed.

The *amigas* exchanged glances, and Carmen, always the most patient of the three, took the lead. "How many people did you want to invite in addition to the two hundred and fifty on your list?" she asked calmly.

"I have to invite my entire sophomore class," Binky replied, as though that were the most reasonable thing in the world. "Just because I'm a Mortimer doesn't make me an elitist. In fact, on the contrary, I'm a woman of the people."

"Well, my understanding is that there are eighty students in your class at Everglades and seventy-eight are already coming. Who are we leaving out?"

Binky began to pace. "My father has very important clients that he wants to have come to this party. Has anyone even bothered to talk to him about his guest list?"

Alicia raised her hand. "I met with your father about his list. He's completely covered."

"Well, I'm not happy with my dress, either," Binky went on. "I want a designer dress, not a *homemade* dress."

The expression on Carmen's face, a mixture of hurt and anger, made it clear that she'd just about had it with Binky's freak-out. But she remained in control. "Believe me, *chica*, I get it. Having a *quinceañera* is stressful. You've got all this pressure on you from your parents, and then you've got a boyfriend whom you've barely gotten comfortable kissing, but now you've got to present him to the world as your *chambelán*. You're learning three different dances. You've got a speech to write and memorize in Spanish."

"What?" Binky screeched. "A speech in Spanish?" She began to cry. "No one told me about making a speech in Spanish."

"Way to go, Carmen," Jamie muttered.

"It's not so much a speech," Carmen backpedaled. "It's more of a formal thank-you."

"In Spanish?" Binky said. "You know I don't speak Spanish."

"Look," Alicia said, "a lot of girls have family in from Mexico, Puerto Rico; even people who live in the Bronx or Chicago, who don't speak English very well or at all. Preparing a few words to say to them in Spanish is a nice touch. But you won't have that kind of family in town. So it might not be necessary. We can discuss and find a compromise. All these things, they're not enough to get this twisted up over. So, tell us what's really going on."

Binky leaned against a gingko tree and began to cry in earnest. She sobbed and heaved, and the others just stood and let her. There was nothing to do, in fact, but let her cry herself out. Finally, when her sobs had become hiccups, she spoke. "I just wish my mom could be here. This is the biggest day of my life, and the only grown-up in my family who understands, even a little bit, is Estrella. Bev doesn't care, and my father just signs the checks. It's not fair. How am I supposed to make this passage to womanhood without the most important woman in my life there?" Binky looked at them, her red-rimmed eyes as if pleading for an answer.

Carmen went over to the distraught girl and gave her a Binky-style bear hug. "Oh, *chica*, I'm so sorry. You're right. It's not fair. But she is going to be with you. She's been with you this whole time. Watching over you."

Alicia gave Binky's shoulder a tight squeeze. "She'd be so proud, I just know it."

In a totally uncharacteristic move, Jamie gave Binky

a hug, too. "Don't worry, B., it might not be the same thing, but you've got three girls here who have your back. We Latinas have to look out for each other."

Binky smiled, looking more like her usual self. "Thank you, guys. I didn't realize when I hired Amigas Inc. that you would be translators, party-planners, cultural guides, dance teachers, *and* therapists all rolled up into one."

"We've got to be," Alicia said as the girls stood up and began to walk back into the offices. "Everyone looks at the pictures and thinks a *quinceañera* is dressing up like a princess and all the fabulosity. But just the fact of presenting yourself to your family and friends as a young woman tends to stir things up emotionally."

"Trust us," Carmen added with a mischievous grin, "Lici nearly lost her mind on our first *quince*."

"And she wasn't even the birthday girl!" Jamie said.

"No me digas," Binky said, pushing Alicia playfully.

"O-o-o-o-o, nice interjection of *español*," Alicia said. "I'm impressed."

"Well, I've learned a thing or *dos o tres*, hanging out with you *chicas*," Binky said saucily, putting her hand on her hip in a Jamie-like stance.

"Okay, okay, enough mocking," Jamie said. "Should I go get Tilda?"

"Sure," Binky agreed. "But *fíjate*, I was serious before. Those cafeteria white plates aren't going to cut it."

Alicia laughed. "We'll look into the Kate Spade. But we're going to have to talk to your dad, because that'll definitely throw us off budget. I'll set up a meeting."

She whipped out her cell phone and secured a five-minute appointment from Mr. Mortimer's secretary.

They were in the hallway of the caterer's office when Jamie pulled Alicia aside.

"Hey, would it be okay if I did the meeting with Mr. Mortimer? Dinner at the country club was a bit of a disaster, and I feel like I owe him an apology."

Alicia frowned. "Disaster? I don't even want to know," she said. "Go ahead and take the meeting. But can you promise me to keep that Jamie-from-the-Bronx temper in check? This is our biggest account ever; I don't want to mess it up."

Jamie nodded. This was something she knew . . . all too well.

Mr. Mortimer's office building was all glass and polished steel. Jamie found herself surprised to be directed to an ordinary bank of elevators. She almost expected a space pod to whisk her up to the thirty-first floor.

Walking into Mr. Mortimer's office, she could tell he

was surprised to see her and not Alicia.

He rose from behind his desk. "Miss Sosa," he said, addressing her as if she were a grown-up, there for a typical business meeting. "I was expecting your colleague, Miss Cruz. Please have a seat."

He directed her to a seating area in which she instantly recognized the expensive black leather Mies van der Rohe club chairs. And the sofa on the edge of which he perched retailed for five grand.

"I wanted to take this meeting because I felt I owed you an in-person apology," Jamie said. "My behavior at the club was out of line. It was not a reflection of the opinions of Amigas Inc. or of my feelings for your son."

Mr. Mortimer was silent for a moment. "I must admit I was taken aback by your choice of outfit that night," he finally said. "I can't imagine what would have led you to believe that it would be appropriate to dress so casually, more casually than I've ever seen you, at our club."

Jamie could feel her face getting hot. While she wanted to put the blame on his wife, she knew she couldn't. She had to own up to her bad behavior.

"I know. And as I said, I'm sorry. It was disrespectful," Jamie said. "But it wasn't what I meant."

Mr. Mortimer turned and went to stand looking

out the window over the Miami skyline. He motioned for her to come and stand next to him. She was fairly certain she'd never seen the city from a vantage point like this. It was spectacular. They stared out, silently pondering.

"I learned a lot from Bianca's mother. It was she who introduced me to Miami and its Latin community," Mr. Mortimer eventually said. "Just as it's a tremendous asset to be bilingual, it's a valuable thing to be bicultural. If you can be just as much at home at a place like the West Side Country Club as you can on Calle Ocho, then you'll have twice as many doors open to you. Do you understand?"

"I think so," she said, hesitantly.

"Yes, the idea of a dress code is a little staid," Mr. Mortimer continued. "But as I'm always telling Bev, it's just clothes. And now I will tell you, it's just a club. And there are rules, but they don't mean you have to change. You just have to bend."

He walked back over to his desk and sat down. "Now, what did Amigas Inc. need?" he asked.

"We wanted to get your budget approval," Jamie said when she found her voice. "Binky would like Kate Spade plates instead of the white plates the caterer provides."

"And how much will that set me back?"

Jamie handed him the estimate.

"That's reasonable," he said after briefly examining it.

"There is just one more thing," she said.

Mr. Mortimer glanced at his watch. "Only if you can be quick. I've got a six p.m."

"I'd like to create something special for Binky's birthday and could use your help."

He looked at her quizzically, and she quickly told him her idea and what she would need. When she had finished, he made a few phone calls and sent a few e-mails.

"Done," he said, finally.

"I think she'll really like it," she said.

"I'm sure she will," he said. "Thank you for being so thoughtful as to give Binky such an incredible gift."

Jamie was surprised at his enthusiasm. Nothing, however, could have prepared her for his walking out from behind his desk and embracing her—in a giant, Binky-style hug.

CHAPTER 15

THE WEST SIDE Country Club felt like a totally different place to Jamie when she arrived that sunny Sunday afternoon. There must have been a hundred kids running around the course with little golf clubs in one hand and cans of golf balls in the other.

For the past two years, Dash had hosted something called the Luz Invitational, where he invited underprivileged kids from all over the city to come to the club. "It's the best day of the year for me," he had told Jamie. "Seeing all those kids running around, laughing and playing and falling in love with golf. It's like Christmas to me. I would love for you to come and see it for yourself. It would mean a lot to me if you were there."

When Jamie found Dash, he looked excited, exhausted, and slightly overwhelmed, like a combination of Dr. Doolittle and Willy Wonka. He was demonstrating a swing to a little girl with thick Coke-bottle glasses as a little boy tried to climb up his back. When he bent down to clean up the divot the little girl had created, two other little boys—on a dare—tickled him, while a third grabbed his cap and took off running.

Jamie watched the scene, amused, until Dash spotted her. Freeing himself and running over, he gave her a quick kiss. "I'm so glad you're here. Listen, I've got to do another demo in five, but I'll see you at lunch. Okay, *querida*?"

"No problem," Jamie said, stealing another kiss. "I can keep myself busy. Where's your sister? I brought the seating charts to go over with her."

"Of course, a party-planner's work is never done." Dash pointed to the pro shop. "Last time I saw her, she was over there, giving out fashion advice."

Saying good-bye, Jamie walked over to the pro shop, where Binky was indeed involved in a fashion undertaking. She was surrounded by a dozen hyperactive-looking girls who looked to be between ten and twelve years old.

"Okay, girls, listen up!" Binky cried, clapping her hands and trying to restore order. "I will buy each of you one outfit. Let me define *outfit*. It's a top, bottom, hat, socks, and shoes."

The girls squealed in delight.

"Or, option number two: dress, cardigan, hat, socks, and shoes. Five pieces. Your choice. But don't be greedy. You cannot take five pairs of sneakers and sell four of them on eBay."

The girls nodded.

"And there's a twist. You've got exactly five minutes to pick what you want and get it to the register," Binky said. "By my clock. On your marks, get ready, set, *go*!"

The girls took off in all directions. Within seconds, the tiny shop looked as if it had been hit by a cyclone.

A tall girl with long hair, an athletic build, and an armload of clothes headed for the dressing room. "You don't have time to try on clothes!" Binky cried.

"But I want to make sure it fits," the girl said shyly.

Binky sighed. "You can always exchange it later. To the register! To the register! You've only got two minutes left."

The girl ran to exchange the shirt, then ran faster when Binky called out, "Sixty seconds . . . Thirty seconds . . . Ten seconds. Okay, you're done."

Binky handed her credit card to the saleswoman, and one by one, each girl was handed a kelly green shopping bag with the club's logo printed on it in white.

Jamie was frowning as she watched the antics, but she didn't know why. She loved free clothes as much as the next girl, but something about Binky's gambit didn't sit right with her.

"Did you see that?" Binky asked when Jamie joined her. "I just did three thousand dollars' worth of good."

Jamie had just figured out what bugged her about the scene. She chose her words carefully. "Did you take time to really connect with any of these girls?"

"They connected with my money, silly. That's what counts."

Jamie sighed. "Is that what you think? Really? The tall girl over there. What's her name? How about the girl with the braids? What does she want to be when she grows up? Six months—no, six *days* from now— you won't remember any of them. And while they may remember your money when they put on their fancy kicks or their country-club polo tops, they won't remember *you*. You're a cool girl, Binky. You've got a big heart. You should let people get close to you, not just close to your pocketbook. You're better than that."

Binky looked stunned for a moment and then said, quietly, "What do you mean by that?"

"Let me show you."

She went over to the saleswoman, asked a few questions, and then called out to the girls, who were beginning to file out of the store. "Wait a second, *chicas*, we're not going back to the golf course yet. We're having a powwow outside. I want you all to get to know the girl who just gave you such lovely gifts— Binky Mortimer."

The saleswoman accommodatingly led the group out to the country-club veranda. It was basically a gigantic, luxurious back porch with huge wicker sofas upholstered in bright, tropical fabrics. Low wooden Balinese tables were piled with board games, playing cards, and coffee-table design books. There was also an exquisite view of the country-club lake and the eighteenth hole.

Jamie ordered a couple of pitchers of lemonade, then encouraged the girls to "sit down, get comfy, and chill out."

Binky took a seat on a sofa next to her. Her hands were clasped tightly on her lap, and she was unusually subdued.

"So, *chicas*, this is the dealio," Jamie began. "Let's get to know each other. Why don't we go around the room and answer two questions: where do you go to school? And . . . what's the name of your crush?"

The girls giggled and blushed.

Jamie pointed to a girl with long, Leona Lewis–style curly hair. "How about you first?"

"My name's Thandie," the girl said shyly. "I go to West Park Elementary. And I have a crush on a boy named Peter."

Jamie clapped, and the other girls joined in.

"Peter, huh?" Jamie said. "Love it! Good luck with *that*!"

The tall girl, who'd wanted to try on her outfit, was next. She said, "My name's Lesley-Ann. I go to Opa Locka Middle School, and I have a crush on a boy named Seth."

The girls all clapped and said, almost in unison, "Seth! Good luck with *that*." They continued around the veranda, revealing their schools and their crushes. One girl bravely admitted to having a crush on another girl, named Penelope.

Then it was Binky's turn.

"Me?" she asked Jamie.

Jamie squeezed her shoulder. "Yep, your turn."

"My name's Bink—" Binky began. "My name's Bianca. I go to Everglades Academy, and I'm crushing on a boy named Tino."

The girls all clapped. "Tino!" they cried in unison. "Good luck with *that*."

Binky laughed and poked Jamie in the ribs. "Okay, smarty-pants. Your turn."

Jamie began to speak, unaware that Dash had come out onto the veranda and was now standing behind her.

"My name is Jamie," she said. "I go to C. G. High, and I have a crush on a boy named Dash."

She almost jumped out of her seat when she heard said crush say, "Good luck with *that*."

As everyone else giggled, he leaned down to kiss her cheek. This prompted the younger girls to start singing, *"Dash and Jamie sitting in a tree. K-I-S-S . . ."*

He held up a hand and they quieted down. "Okay, okay, we know how that song goes. I actually came over to tell you all that lunch is being served."

As the girls stood up to leave, each of them came over and gave Jamie and Binky hugs.

When Lesley-Ann approached, Binky gave her an extralong hug. "I apologize for rushing you in the store before," she said sincerely. "Come find me after lunch; we'll make sure you get the size you need."

Dash squeezed Jamie's shoulder. "Looks like you and Binky made some new friends."

"Actually, it's 'Bianca,'" his sister said, turning to look at him. "That's my name, after all."

Dash nodded. "Bianca, huh? I'm going to have to get used to that."

She smiled. "I think you can manage. You're a pretty

smart guy. Mind if I keep your girlfriend for a second more?"

"We'll meet you in the dining room," Jamie said.

"No shopping detours," Dash warned, racing off to catch up with the other girls, who were headed toward the dining room.

Binky and Jamie walked down the veranda steps. "Thanks for this," Binky said finally.

Jamie shrugged. "No biggie."

"It *was* a biggie. You know everybody always wants Dash to give speeches about his golf career, his life on and off the green. I never thought that anybody would want to hear me talk. Or that I had anything much to offer, besides money."

Jamie looked at Binky and realized how fragile she really was. Something clicked. She knew that feeling well. It reminded her of being at boarding school. After all this time of thinking they were so different, she and Binky were, well, alike.

"Well, now, you can see how wrong you are," Jamie said gently. "Let people get to know you, Bianca. They won't be disappointed."

"I think the same could be said of you, Jamie from the Bronx," she said. "You weren't exactly warm and fuzzy when we first met, *chica*. My dad always says that we teach what we need to learn. So, you know, I'm here, if you ever want to talk."

"Point taken," Jamie said. "And thanks."

"Now, I'd better get you to lunch before my brother kills me," Binky said.

"What? No Binky bear hug?" Jamie asked.

Binky threw her arms around the other girl. "You mean, *Bianca* bear hug."

"Right," Jamie said, laughing. "You know it's going to take us all a minute to get used to calling you by your real name."

The girl looked down at her name tag, which still said BINKY in large block letters. "I could start by changing this," she said sheepishly.

"Excellent idea," Jamie said. Then, hooking elbows, she and Binky took off toward the country-club dining room.

CHAPTER 16

LATER THAT NIGHT, Jamie was editing a video on her laptop in the studio when Dash called.

"Hey, what are you doing?" he asked.

"Depends." Jamie asked "What are you doing?"

She loved the way that even the most basic conversations had romantic overtones when you were falling in love with someone. It had taken this relationship with Dash to make Jamie understand the meaning of the term *sweet nothings*. She could've talked to Dash about the weather, the size and shape of the Venetian blinds in her studio, the number of stitches in his golf shoes—and she would have been perfectly happy and entertained.

"I'm talking to my girlfriend," he teased. "Listen, I've got a big game coming up, and I was hoping you could come."

"I think I can do that," Jamie said. "When is it?"

"This Friday," Dash answered. "The twenty-sixth."

Jamie's pulse quickened. Friday was the day after Thanksgiving, so there was no school. But it was also the day *before* Binky's *quince*, officially known among the members of Amigas Inc. as *Quince* Eve. And while on Christmas Eve you generally spent a quiet evening at home with your family, wrapping presents, eating yummy food, and anticipating the big day, things were different on *Quince* Eve, which meant running around putting out fires and, more often than not, dealing with a late night full of last-minute details. Alicia and Carmen would *kill* her if she skipped any of it. Maybe if she promised to pull an all-nighter . . .

"I'll be there." The words were out of her mouth before she could stop them. How long could a golf game last, anyway? She'd be away from her Amigas duties for four hours, tops.

"Awesome," he went on. "I leave for Palm Beach Thursday, but my father and Binky are coming up for the day. I was hoping you'd come up with them."

"Palm Beach, wow. That's far away," Jamie said. "For some reason I thought it would be a nearby thing. I kinda was supposed to work."

"Totally; I get it. Work trumps cheering your boyfriend on. Your poor, sad, lonely boyfriend, who might just blow the biggest game of his life, because he will be missing you . . ."

Jamie caved.

"I'm *so* coming with you," she said, beaming into the phone.

"That's more like it. And to thank you, we'll have dinner at the Breakers afterwards," Dash said. "Hopefully, it'll be a victory dinner."

The next day, Jamie dashed into Bongos for a meeting with Carmen and Alicia. She had called them and told them that they had to talk, but not told them why. She'd dressed for the event in a Lilly Pulitzer dress with a pair of fishnet tights and hot pink combat boots.

"Preppy much?" Alicia asked when Jamie slid into the booth where they were waiting.

"Yeah, I never figured you for the Lilly type," Carmen agreed.

"It was a gift from Dash, and I kinda dig it," Jamie said. "I put my own spin on it with the fishnets and the boots."

"Like it," Carmen said, nodding.

"Me, too," Alicia said. "It's unexpected; that's cool."

Jamie just wanted to spill, but before she could, she had to wait for the usual catching up, a few minutes of *quince* talk, and then a few more of deciding on food. Finally, after the tapas and snacks were ordered, Jamie broke her big news.

"I've got to go to Palm Beach on Friday to see Dash play in a championship match," she said, the words tumbling out of her mouth like bumper cars with no brakes.

Carmen and Alicia exchanged glances. They were silent. Until . . .

"Are you kidding?" Alicia shouted.

"That's *Quince* Eve!" Carmen cried, horrified.

"It just that Dash has this huge match. . . ." Jamie began.

"And *we*—as in, *your partners*—have got this huge party to throw," Alicia pointed out snippily.

"Well, technically, you could look at it as part of work," Jamie said tentatively. "I figure that spending two hours in the car with Binky—I mean, Bianca—is a good way to calm her nerves the day before the big event."

Carmen and Alicia weren't buying it. "What about the nerves of her twenty-four relatives who are flying in from all over the country—and Venezuela—who need to be picked up at the airport and greeted at the hotel with maps and welcome baskets?"

Jamie took a deep breath. She tried a different, slightly less honest approach. "I have no choice, you guys. Mr. Mortimer himself personally requested my attendance."

"Come on, Jamie, let's keep it real," Alicia said. "There's a yachtload of work to do, and you just want to blow it off so you can take a road trip with your boyfriend. The boyfriend, I might add, whom you never tell us anything about and who has seemingly changed you—a lot."

Jamie felt as if she'd been slapped. She had known that Carmen and Alicia would be mad at her, but she had hoped they would cut her some slack this time. She always pulled her own weight. Binky's *quinceañera* was no exception.

She took a deep breath, trying not to lose her cool completely. "I'm asking for eight hours off, that's all. And I don't complain when I'm alone in my studio at all hours, pouring sand through a funnel into two hundred and fifty message-in-a-bottle invitations. How about this? I'll do all the welcome baskets by Thursday. Then I'll have the Mortimers' driver take me to the hotel so I can drop off baskets and maps for the guests before we leave on the trip."

Carmen shook her head. "Alicia's right, *chica*. I don't know what's gotten into you. First you're all Bronx and anti–rich girl. Then it's like you're the Bride of

Golfenstein and you're wearing country-club dresses and talking about having the Mortimers' driver do your work for you."

Jamie fought to blink back the tears, but it was impossible. They started flowing, and once they started, they wouldn't stop.

"You guys are being so mean right now," she said through her sobs. "Do you think it felt good all those times I was the fifth wheel to your perfectly matched sets? Alicia, you had Gaz. Carmen, you had Domingo. And now I've *finally* met someone, and I'm so so happy. Isn't my happiness bigger than one day of errands?" She picked up her purse and put ten dollars down on the table, payment for food she wasn't staying to eat. "It's okay," she said. "You don't have to answer, because I've already decided. Being happy, being in love—finally— is bigger to me than Amigas Inc. Consider this my notice. I quit." She rushed out, bumping into Domingo on the way.

"Hey," he said, grabbing her arm. "Everything okay?"

"It's not," Jamie said. "But it will be."

Back in the restaurant, Alicia and Carmen were in shock. "She's gone off the deep end!" Alicia said, laughing hollowly.

"It's like she got hit in the head with a five iron," Carmen said.

They paused and looked at each other.

"We weren't too hard on her, were we?" Alicia asked hesitantly.

Carmen shook her head. "She shouldn't have ditched us at the last minute, boyfriend or not. *Quinces* are a huge amount of work. Nobody knows that more than Jamie."

Jamie took the bus to her favorite consignment shop, So Five Minutes Ago. She needed to clear her head. She felt better the minute she opened the door and heard the familiar bell clang.

The owner of the store, Aerin Lauper, was ringing up a customer, so Jamie just waved hello and began browsing.

When Aerin was done, she came over. Aerin had grown up in Hawaii, the daughter of a Korean mom and a German dad. She put a plastic lei around Jamie's neck. The Hawaiian welcome was part of what made her shop so popular.

"*Maholo*, Jamie, what kind of *quince* magic are you trying to make today?" Aerin asked.

Jamie looked down at her hands. "Well, actually,

today, I'm looking for me. I've got some credit for the Air Jordans I sold you a few months back, right?"

Aerin laughed. "Are you kidding? You could buy half the store for what those Jordans are worth."

"Excellent," Jamie said. "I want to get some more dresses like this." She pointed at what she was wearing. "And maybe some kitten heels."

"Busting out a new look, huh? The Bronx meets Jackie O. I like it." Aerin said.

"Something like that. I've got this new boyfriend, and he's a big-time golf player, and I'm feeling in need of a change."

"Most of the girls who come in here want to change their look *after* they break up, not when they first start dating." The older woman began walking through the racks, deftly pulling out argyle cardigans, pastel polos, and ice-cream-colored miniskirts in Jamie's size.

"Well, you could say that I'm breaking up and falling in love with a new guy at the same time," Jamie said. She explained how she'd quit Amigas Inc. and was going to focus all of her attention on her art and her relationship with Dash.

"But you love planning *quinces*," Aerin pointed out.

"I know, I just . . ." Jamie could feel the tears coming again. "I just need a break, that's all."

"You didn't ask for my advice, but you remind me so much of myself when I was your age that I've got to give it: don't just do the country-club prep thing without putting your own spin on it. I think this makeover needs a little more Latin flavor."

"What do you have in mind?" Jamie said, studying her reflection in the dressing-room mirror. "I'm game for changing *everything*."

CHAPTER 17

ON FRIDAY MORNING, Jamie had awakened with a start. At Aerin's suggestion, she'd completed her clothing makeover with a new hairdo. The girl who now stared back at her in the bathroom mirror had Shakira-style dirty blond locks.

Her first impulse was to take a picture of herself with her cell phone and e-mail it to Alicia and Carmen. But as neither of her best friends had spoken to her since the Bongos blow-out, she didn't think the update would be much appreciated. Instead, she changed her profile picture and status on Facebook, asking the question: Is it true that *rubias* have more fun?

Aware that the last time she had gone out with the Mortimers her style choices had left something to be desired, she dressed carefully for the big match. She wore a strapless red and white Baby Phat dress, a red varsity cardigan with white stripes on the cuffs, and a pair of vintage-look red Miu-Miu wedge heels. She glanced at the image in the mirror. "A little uptown, a little downtown, a hundred percent me," she said to her reflection.

Ferris was waiting in front of her house with the Mortimers' car. When she appeared, he jumped out and opened the door for her.

"Hiya, Ferris," she said. Peering inside the empty car, she asked, "Where are Bianca and her dad?"

"They decided to go up yesterday to see Dash's early round," the driver explained. "I hope you don't mind."

"No problem," Jamie said. Tentatively she added, "It's still kind of early in the morning for me. Would it be okay if I took a nap in the backseat on our ride up?" It was less that she was tired and more that by sleeping she could forget that she was ditching her girls—*had* ditched them.

"But of course," Ferris replied. "I keep a silk pillow and a cashmere blanket in the trunk for exactly such occasions."

Jamie found herself thinking, not for the first time, I could get used to this.

She woke up just as the car pulled into downtown Palm Beach. It reminded her a little of South Beach in its scale and architecture, but the people here were older, tanner, and wearing about ten times as much bling.

When they arrived at the golf course, Jamie was surprised to see hundreds of people milling around outside the front gate. It was what she might have expected to see at an arena-rock concert, not at a golf tournament. Even after she'd fallen for Dash, she'd remained fairly confident that golf was to professional sports what Latin was to modern languages—obscure and obsolete. This crowd was proving her wrong.

Ferris looked back at Jamie in the rearview mirror. "It can get pretty rowdy in there. Should I park the car and escort you to the VIP section?"

Jamie shook her head. "I think I can manage. Thanks."

Ferris handed her a laminated pass that read: PALM BEACH CLASSIC, JUNIOR CHAMPIONSHIPS, ALL ACCESS. Then he wished her luck and gave her his cell-phone number in case she got lost or needed his help.

Jamie thanked him and left the car. She'd been trying, ever since she met him, to figure out who it was that he reminded her of, and now it hit her: Alfred, in the Batman movies. Like Batman's confidant, Ferris was efficient, British, sensitive, and smart. The thought made her smile.

Jamie made her way through the crowd, surprised at its diversity. Maybe most of the players were white men, but the fans seemed to come from every walk of life. It took her a full twenty minutes to wend her way through the throng to the VIP section, where she spotted Binky and her dad.

"Whoa! I barely recognized you," Binky said when Jamie walked up. "I like your dark roots—very rock-and-roll. Have the others seen the new style?"

"Um, no, and, well, I felt like I needed a change." Apparently Alicia and Carmen were keeping quiet about Jamie's departure from the group. She was on the point of breaking the news when Mr. Mortimer smiled approvingly and said, "Change can be good." After that, the moment seemed to have passed.

Growing more and more comfortable by the minute, Jamie relaxed and began to look around. The fairways were so green and perfectly manicured that they looked movie-set fake. The golfers and caddies, dressed in their classic hats, pants, and shoes, were almost too well coordinated to be true. And Jamie was fairly certain that she'd never seen so much plaid in her life. What she didn't see was the reason she'd gotten up at the crack of dawn and driven three hours to be there.

"Where's Dash?" she asked.

Binky nodded toward the right. "Press box."

Looking in that direction, Jamie saw him, talking to a group of reporters. He seemed absolutely unfazed by all the cameras or the mikes that were thrust two inches from his mouth. He looked as comfortable answering questions from complete strangers as he had talking to Jamie that very first night at Ojos Así.

At that moment, he looked up, caught her eye, and tugged at his hair. Jamie wasn't an expert at reading lips, but she thought it looked as if he were mouthing, *What's up?*

She gave her hair a shampoo-commercial-worthy toss and waved. There'd be time to fill him in later.

Play started, and almost immediately, Jamie realized that she had narrowly averted making a huge mistake. She thanked the shoe gods that she was wearing a pair of wedges and not the stilettos she'd initially pulled out of her closet. How was she to know, when she'd gotten up at six in the morning, that in golf, the fans followed the players, rather than sitting in the bleachers looking cute, the way they did in tennis. She also hadn't known how quiet everything—and everyone—would be.

"What am I looking at?" she whispered to Binky as they walked along the first hole. "Explain the basics to me."

Binky shrugged. "Besides the fact that each of the guys are trying to get the ball in the hole in as few moves as possible, I don't know much. Mostly, I just try to stay hydrated and gorgeous."

As they followed Dash to the next hole, Jamie tried to get Mr. Mortimer's take on what was going on.

"Oh, it's a magnificent game," Mr. Mortimer said. "I consider it on a level with a martial art, for its combination of mental acuity, strength, and speed."

Jamie had a hard time making the connection between golf and karate, but she went with it.

"One of the things that makes Dash so good is his strength; he opens so strong," Mr. Mortimer went on. "He averages more than three hundred yards off of the tee."

Jamie had no idea what that meant, exactly, but she got the feeling it meant Dash was very, very good.

"Did you teach him to play, Mr. Mortimer?" she asked in a whisper.

The question made Dash's dad smile. "I started bringing him to the club with me when he was just a toddler," he said. "One year, when Dash couldn't have been much older than three, a client gave him a tiny little set of golf clubs as a Christmas gift. Ever since then, no toy, no food, no TV show ever interested him as much as this game. That is, until he met you."

Jamie blushed. Surely, Mr. Mortimer was just flattering her. But why would he need to? If anything, one would have imagined that he'd have done just the opposite, trying to keep the Bronx girl away from his rich and increasingly famous son.

She was trying to figure out the perfect response— *I really like your son, too*, or maybe, *I quit my job with Amigas Inc. to be here today; that's how crazy I am about Dash*—when the unthinkable happened. Her cell phone rang. In the middle of all that silence.

Dash had been just about to make the putt, and according to the press accounts that would later appear, it was an easy one. But Jamie's ringing phone distracted him. He missed the shot.

All of a sudden, hundreds of eyes were on her, and because her giant purse was a bottomless pit, it took five full rings for her to find the phone and turn it off.

"Sorry," Jamie whispered, looking at Dash. She apologized to Binky, Mr. Mortimer, and everybody else who was within earshot.

Luckily, her ringing phone didn't in the end cost Dash the game. She wasn't sure exactly how it was that he finally sealed the championship, as she kept her head down for the rest of the play. But as Mr. Mortimer explained it, "Dash crushed the tee shot for a third straight birdie, and that gave him control of the match."

After his final putt on the eighteenth hole, Dash pulled Jamie out of the crowd and gave her a big hug.

"Thank you for coming," he whispered, holding her close.

"Thank *you* for winning," she whispered back.

He laughed. "Thank you for turning off your cell phone before my big game. . . . Oh, wait, you didn't do that."

Jamie cringed. "Okay, okay, my bad."

"Next time," Dash said, in a teasing tone, "maybe leave your cell in the car with Ferris."

She shivered at his words. Next time. There would definitely be a next time.

As they walked back to the club so Dash could shower and change, he ran his fingers through her hair. "It's different," he observed.

"Different good or different bad?" she said.

"I think different good," he said. "But I find myself wondering who the real Jamie is."

She squeezed his hand and said, "You know what? For a long time, I was so into representing the boogie-down Bronx and playing the game that I think I got stuck in something that wasn't real. I'm not sure who the real Jamie is, either. But I'm having fun figuring it out. Do you think I look like I'm faking it?"

Dash kissed her on the lips and said, "There's absolutely nothing fake about you, Jamie Sosa."

CHAPTER 18

THAT NIGHT, Jamie joined Dash and a posse of his family and golf friends for a victory dinner at the Breakers Hotel in Palm Beach. The group sat at a giant table on the patio overlooking the water. A waiter poured pitchers of Dash's favorite drink, the Arnold Palmer—half lemonade, half iced tea—a drink that was named after the legendary golfer.

A trio of waiters brought out the first course: stone crab claws with drawn butter, fried oysters on the half shell, and huge piles of jumbo shrimp with cocktail sauce.

Sitting next to Dash, his hand firmly held in hers, Jamie looked out onto the water and marveled that so much had changed in her life in such a short time. A month ago, she had had no idea that she would meet an amazing guy and travel to another city with him, dye her hair blond, or become the most unlikely golf fan in the state of Florida.

A month ago, she also couldn't have imagined that her friendships with Alicia and Carmen would be on life support. She wondered what they were doing just then. She was having lots of fun, but it *was* Quince Eve. There was a ton of work still left to do for Binky's event the next day. Stuff she should have been helping with.

With alarm, she realized that she needed to get back to Miami, make up with her friends, and set things right immediately.

Jamie leaned over to Dash. "I'm so sorry, but I've got to go."

Dash looked surprised. "Stay. My dad will get you and Binky a hotel room. Ferris will drive you back first thing in the morning. The *quince* isn't until three p.m. There's plenty of time."

Jamie resisted the urge to give in. "I wish I could, but I've really got to get back."

Dash grinned. "You're kind of making this a habit, leaving dinner early."

Jamie shrugged. "At least this time, I don't look like the Latina Lady Gaga, and I got to finish my salad."

The drive from Palm Beach to Miami was three hours plus, even without traffic. As soon as Ferris had gotten on the highway, Jamie fell asleep. She awoke with a start when they were almost home.

She looked at her watch. It was almost midnight, and the Miami skyline still shimmered in the distance ahead. It was late, she was exhausted, and she really wasn't in the mood to be dissed. But she also knew that she wouldn't be able to go to sleep until things were put right again.

"Ferris, would it be okay if we made a couple of stops before you took me home?" she asked.

Ferris tilted his charcoal gray chauffeur's cap back. "Not a problem with me, Miss Sosa. But I suggest that you call your parents and advise them that we are running late."

Jamie snapped her fingers. Right. Parents. Out past midnight. Calling was a great idea. She'd only known him a few weeks, but already Ferris was saving her butt. As much as she had once criticized Alicia, and more recently Binky, for being rich, she was beginning to think less disdainfully of money—and the people who had it. Dash, his father, and his sister had shown her that having a kajillion dollars didn't automatically turn you into a Mrs. Mortimer–style jerk. That had been a big *aha* moment. But on a more practical level, spending all this time with Ferris and being driven around in the

Mortimers' car had shown her that being spoiled by things like a car and driver was *definitely* something she could get used to. But that particular secret, for the time being, was going to go no further than the luxuriously appointed leather interiors of the Maybach's incredibly comfy back seat.

Jamie called her parents, explaining that although it was late, it was *Quince* Eve and she still had a couple of pressing work matters to attend to. After getting Ferris's assurance that he would bring her home safely, Jamie's mom let her go.

With that taken care of, Jamie gave Ferris directions to the Cruz home. Once they had hit Miami proper, they were able to get there within minutes. When they arrived, she handed him her iPod and asked if he could plug it into the converter and pump up the volume. Her plan was to blast One Republic's "I Apologize" outside Alicia's house until she'd made her point. In junior high, she and Alicia had sung the classic pop song at dozens of karaoke sleepovers. Remembering the soulful lyrics and all the fun they'd had together over the years, Jamie felt certain that Alicia would have no choice but to take her back into the group.

But Ferris wasn't having it. He explained that the city of Miami had very strict ordinances against noise late at night in residential neighborhoods.

"While I've grown very fond of you, Miss Sosa," he said, "there is no way I will risk a thousand-dollar fine and the besmirching of the Mortimer name for a potentially disastrous stunt."

It was probably just that she was very tired, but Jamie began to cry. She was fresh out of ideas, and she needed to get back in with her friends.

"What should I do, Ferris?" she sniffed. "I've messed everything up."

He didn't seem put out by this display of emotion—he did, after all, work full-time for the Mortimers. After considering the question for a few moments, he said, "Why don't you call your friend on her cell phone? Invite her to come talk to you in the car. Most people have never sat inside a vehicle like this one, and I will play the song *inside,* where only the three of us can hear it."

While this plan didn't have as much dramatic panache as hers had, Jamie was willing to give it a try. She dialed Alicia's number.

Moments later, Alicia was standing outside. If the state of her hair was any indication, she'd been fast asleep when Jamie called.

Rubbing her eyes vigorously in an attempt to wake

up, Alicia asked, "What do you want, Jamie?"

"Come inside the car," Jamie said in a whisper—although there was no one in the driveway—or on the street, for that matter—to be disturbed.

As Alicia got into the backseat of the car, Ferris began to play the song. She smiled and said sleepily, "They're playing our song. Where's the karaoke mike?"

"I'll have one next time. Promise," Jamie said, relieved that her friend wasn't brushing her off.

Waking up a little, Alicia looked around. "Is this a Maybach?"

Jamie was incredulous. "How'd you know?"

"It's my brother's dream car. He's got a picture of this exact model on his bedroom wall. He figures he only has to raise, like, a gazillion dollars to afford one. But you didn't wake me up to talk cars, did you?"

Jamie took a deep breath. "No. I woke you up to apologize. I'm sorry I've been such a flaky friend. I'm kind of going through some changes."

Alicia grinned. "No kidding. Blond much?"

Jamie self-consciously patted her hair. She'd forgotten all about coloring it. "I was going for the Shakira look—blond for more fun, black roots . . ."

"—To stay *true* to your roots?" Alicia asked.

"I was going to say, to give it that rock-and-roll edge," Jamie said. "But enough about my hair. I promise to work like a dog all night—well, the rest of the night, anyway, which is actually already tomorrow—to make Bianca's *quince* the best one we've ever done. Can you accept my apology?"

Alicia groaned. "Fine, fine. But please don't tell me that the *quince* is today."

"It is," Jamie said, brightly.

"Welcome back," Alicia said, giving her friend a hug. "It's only been a day, but we missed you."

"Me, too," Jamie said. "Now I'm going to go and apologize to Carmen."

"What are you going to do? You can't drive a car onto her street."

"This I know from experience," Ferris chimed in.

"And she hates any song by One Republic," Alicia said.

"I'll think of something," Jamie said. "Good night. I'll see you in the morning."

After waiting to make sure that Alicia was safely back inside her house, Jamie and Ferris made a quick stop at Jamie's studio. Then they drove to Carmen's. It was one in the morning by the time Jamie called her on her cell phone.

"You'd better have a really good excuse for waking me up in the middle of the night, Sosa," Carmen said grumpily.

Jamie could feel her heart beating wildly. Making up with Alicia had been easy. She hadn't been prepared for softhearted Carmen to be so hard-hearted.

"I'm sorry. I mean, I just really needed to talk to you. I know it's late. Just look outside your window," Jamie said.

She got out of the car and stood on the footbridge in front of Carmen's house, flashing an industrial-size light onto the giant white tarp she'd gotten at her studio. On it, she'd written in spray paint: FORGIVE ME.

Carmen was standing on the balcony of her family's house, and Jamie could barely see her in the dark, but she could hear her friend's laughter on the other end of the line.

"You know you're crazy, right?" Carmen said.

"I'm sorry we had a falling-out, but I plan to make it up to you tomorrow, by being the busiest *quince*-worker-bee you've ever seen," Jamie said.

"Um okay," Carmen said, "but if you miss a *Quince* Eve again . . ."

"No lo digas," Jamie said. "Don't even say it, because it's not going to happen. See you tomorrow, okay?"

"Wait a second," Carmen said. "What's going on with your hair?"

Jamie nearly dropped her cell phone into the canal. "You can see all the way from over there? It's so freaking dark outside!"

"I can see you perfectly fine," Carmen said. "Is your hair blond now?"

Jamie grew a little nervous. "Um, yeah. But I have no idea how you could know that."

"Alicia called to tell me," Carmen said, starting to guffaw.

"So you were just *pretending* to be asleep?" Jamie asked, not believing it.

"Uh-huh," Carmen said.

"That's wicked," Jamie said.

"So is missing *Quince* Eve," Carmen said.

"Fair enough," Jamie laughed. "But no make-up latte and doughnuts for you."

"I can live with those terms," Carmen said. "See you tomorrow, Sosa."

A few minutes later, Jamie's cell phone rang. It was Carmen.

"On second thought, I think you'd better bring me the make-up latte and the doughnuts," she said.

Jamie laughed. "Done," she said.

CHAPTER 19

AT THE CRACK of dawn the next morning, as promised, Jamie was back on the job. She was functioning on only a few hours' sleep, but she was determined to make it up to her friends for dropping the ball the day before.

Binky had decided to give each of her guests a Prada beach towel, which had to be the priciest party favor ever. Because she'd left this decision until the very last moment, however, special arrangements had had to made with the Prada store to pick them up at the warehouse at six a.m. Since Ferris had gone home to get some much-needed sleep, Jamie got a ride to the warehouse from her dad.

The Sosas' family car was also the one that Davide used for his car-service business, a late-model navy town car. Jamie looked over at her father admiringly.

She really liked being whisked around town by Ferris in one of the Mortimers' fancy cars, but she *loved* sitting in the front seat of her father's car and seeing the city through his eyes. They didn't get to do it nearly enough.

It took her and her father more than half an hour to load all the boxes. They filled up the trunk and the entire backseat. Then Davide dropped her off at Alicia's so she could get to work. "Have fun," he said, kissing her on the forehead.

"Please, Papa," she said, gesturing to the big stack of boxes piled behind her on Alicia's sidewalk. "Fun's got nothing to do with it."

And she wasn't kidding. Binky and her father wanted each beach towel to be rolled up and placed in a canvas "Mortimer Industries" tote. Jamie was to tie each bag with an orange ribbon and attach a card embossed with the guest's name.

Jamie dragged the boxes to the backyard and set up an assembly line near the pool. But even with some help (and snacks) from Maribelle, the Cruz family cook, it still took her more than two hours to bag and tag all those beach towels.

When they were all loaded in the Amigas Inc. van, Maribelle came and put a hand on her shoulder. "*Ay,* Jamie," she said, "you look exhausted. How about you lie down in the Florida room for a quick nap?"

Jamie shook her head. "Thanks, Maribelle, but I don't have the time. There's too much to do."

She did manage to grab a snack, though, and then she took the bus to Carmen's, where she waited as Carmen hand-steamed all the wrinkles out of Binky's gown. Then Jamie took the dress via taxi to the loading dock where the Mortimer yacht was being prepped for the big celebration. She hung the dress up in Binky's room on the boat and looked enviously at the bed. But she knew she could not think about sleep. She had to keep moving.

Binky wanted each of her *damas* to wear a silver bracelet with a sailboat charm on it, and these had been ordered. So Jamie got back on the bus and headed to the jewelry store to pick the seven bracelets up. As the salesperson double-checked each box to make sure the bracelet inside was exactly perfect, Jamie looked on admiringly. They were beautiful. But she had no time to window-shop, because as soon as she'd secured the *damas'* bracelets, she had to run all the way to the opposite side of town to pick up ships'-wheel cuff links for Binky's *chambelanes*. She was standing in the men's shop, waiting for the cuff links to be wrapped, when her cell phone rang. It was Gaz. While he hadn't been partaking in the nitty-gritty of planning, he was still the music man in charge.

"I have a crisis," Gaz said when she picked up. "My mutt dog, Lucinda W., ate the sheet music for the father-daughter *vals*. Alicia said you were downtown, and I was hoping that you could run over to Manny's and pick up another set for me and the guys in the band."

"I can do that," Jamie said.

"You're a lifesaver," Gaz said, hanging up.

Five seconds later, her phone rang again. Without even looking at the number, she answered it.

"*Quince*-crisis help line; this is Jamie. How can I help you?" she said.

"Oh, my God," Binky said. "It's like you read my mind. I'm having a huge crisis. *Huge!*"

"Well, what can I do for you?" Jamie asked, mouthing *Thank you* to the salesperson and walking out onto the street.

"My cousin isn't coming to my *quince*!" Binky cried. "Her plane is stuck in Denver. There's a massive snowstorm. Can you believe that? On *my quince*!"

"Hold on one minute, B.," Jamie replied. She flagged down a cab and slid into the backseat, juggling the bags and her cell phone. "In nearly every other part of the

United States, it's winter," Jamie said calmly. "And in winter, it snows."

"Duh, I know that," Binky said, sounding exasperated on the other side of the line. "What I mean is, why would she fly commercial on my big day? A private jet pilot would've been able to circumvent such a catastrophe. *What. Ever.* The point is, will you be one of my *damas*?"

Jamie tried to keep the groan out of her reply. "Binky, I have a million things to do, and each and every one of them is for your *quince*."

Binky seemed unimpressed. "So, do them, and when the boat leaves the dock, change into the dress and show me what a stand-up *dama* you can be."

"I guess I can do that," Jamie said.

"Of course you can. *Muchas gracias, mi amiga,*" Binky said, clicking off.

Just as soon as Jamie had hung up, the phone rang yet again. What did Binky want now? Determined to be cheerful, Jamie once again answered with: "*Quince*-crisis help line; this is Jamie. How can I help you?"

"Well," said a deep voice that was definitely not Binky's, "I miss my girlfriend something awful. Do you think you can help me with that?"

Dash.

"I have it on good authority that you'll be seeing your girlfriend at three p.m. today," Jamie said soothingly.

"Two hours." Dash sighed. "I guess I can wait."

It couldn't be one o'clock already! Jamie thought. It couldn't be two hours until the Mortimer *quince* kickoff!

"Dash, I adore you, and I can't wait to see you, but I've really got to go," Jamie said, totally panicked.

Two stressful hours later, Jamie was standing in front of the Mortimers' boat with Carmen and Alicia, checking guests in for Binky's *quinceañera*. It seemed unnecessary to the group that the entrance to the boat be guarded with a velvet rope and a professional nightclub bouncer, but what did they know? They were just there to make sure Binky got exactly what she wanted—OTT or not.

"Hi, welcome to Bianca's *quince*," Jamie greeted each guest as he or she arrived.

Then Carmen outfitted them with plastic bracelets, and Alicia stamped their hands with a special mark visible only under black lights.

"You know, those markers are only to let people in and out of nightclubs," said Rick, the bouncer they had pulled away from his other duties for one night.

"We know," the girls said in unison.

"I doubt anyone will be getting on and off the boat once we're out on the water," Rick said.

"We know," the girls repeated.

A few yards away, Tilda Fales directed the catering trucks as they loaded the prepared food onto the boat. She made her way over to where the *amigas* were standing.

"I was just thinking earlier today that you three never get to enjoy any of the gorgeous food I make for these events," she said. "What if I have the chefs make you each up a plate, and when you get a quiet moment, we'll bring them out to you?"

"Fabulous," Jamie said. "You're the best, Tilda."

"I'm always *so* hungry," Carmen said. "Thank you."

"No worries," Tilda said. "I know how it goes. A *quince* planner's job is never done."

When the last guest had boarded, the three made sure they were good to go and then joined Binky's family and friends and the birthday girl herself on the deck of the ship, throwing confetti as the boat pulled away from the dock. All of a sudden, Jamie remembered something.

"The photographer is late and is going to catch a

ferry out to the boat," she said. "But that means no one is taking pictures of the confetti departure!"

"I should have hired a backup photographer," Alicia groaned, hitting herself on the forehead. "This is a mess."

"Maybe not," Jamie said. She took her phone out of her purse and tossed it down to the Mortimers' driver, who was standing on the dock and waving good-bye. "Hey, Ferris, catch! Take lots of pictures!"

Ferris dived for the phone. He gave Jamie a thumbs-up and began to snap photos wildly.

Alicia laughed. "Are you nuts? It took you six months to save for that phone. What if he hadn't caught it?"

Jamie just smiled and said, "I wasn't worried. Ferris is the man. He hasn't let me down yet."

CHAPTER 20

IT WAS SUNSET, and Miami was miles away, when Binky Mortimer's *quinceañera* began in earnest. Gaz and his brothers had been playing old MTV hits for more than an hour, and the guests had been dancing away on the party deck, which had been specially outfitted for the occasion with a checkerboard dance floor and a raised stage for Gaz's band. But now it was time to slow things down and partake in the church ceremony.

The Amigas crew led the guests to the admiral's deck, where formal seating had been set up in the open-air lounge and the guests could enjoy 360-degree views of the water.

Alicia then escorted Padre Alfonso—all six wiry, handsome feet of him—to the front of the ship and willed herself not to call him Padre Hottie when she announced him.

Once the guests were seated, Binky, her father,

and her stepmother moved forward. The *damas* and *chambelanes* stood in a horseshoe formation behind her—seven *damas* to her right, seven *chambelanes* to her left. Jamie, who was dressed in her own navy floor-length *dama* dress, winked at Alicia and gave a little wave to Carmen, who stood at the back of the seating area, ready to help any guests who might need her.

"Ladies and gentlemen," the priest began, "we are gathered here today to celebrate the fifteenth birthday of Bianca Camilla Mortimer. The *quinceañera* tradition dates back more than six hundred years and has its roots in the coming-of-age rituals of the Aztecs and the Mayans. Over the years, the celebration has taken many forms, but its aim always remains the same—to welcome our girls as young women of faith into the church community, into the Latin community, and into our American communities at large. Please join me in prayer."

Padre Alfonso closed his eyes to say a prayer, but every girl in the room kept her eyes open, the better to take his handsomeness in. Then he said, "Now it's the time for us to present Bianca with the traditional gifts."

"Oh, yeah!" Binky squealed. "Let the gifts begin!"

The entire crowd laughed.

The priest smiled. "This first gift may be something

that Bianca, being as humble as she is, would want to wear. It's the tiara."

Bev Mortimer stepped forward and placed the tiara on Binky's head. "The tiara symbolizes the fact that you are a princess in the eyes of God," the priest said. "The next gift is the bracelet."

Dash stepped forward and put a gold tennis bracelet on his sister's wrist.

"The bracelet," Padre Alfonso explained, "symbolizes the unbroken circle of God's love. And there is one more gift—a pair of earrings—to remind you to listen to the words of God."

Chip Mortimer stepped forward. "These earrings belonged to your mother, Bianca," he said, his voice full of emotion. "She was wearing them the evening that I met her. Now, watching you—after all the changes that have taken place since you started this journey to plan a *quince* and connect with your Latin roots—I feel like I'm meeting . . ."

Tears welled up in his eyes, and he struggled to compose himself. He turned away from the group, took a deep breath, hugged her, and continued. "I feel like I'm meeting my grown-up daughter for the first time. Happy birthday, Bianca."

He handed her the earrings and she put them

on. Then she flashed the crowd a big smile, her eyes glittering with happy tears that were almost as sparkly as the diamonds. With this phase of the ceremony complete, Padre Alfonso said a closing prayer and then asked the group to join Binky and her father on the lower deck for the father-daughter *vals*.

It took a while to get the crowd of people onto the second level, but when everyone was assembled, Carmen dimmed the lights and Alicia handed Mr. Mortimer a microphone.

"Before I dance with my daughter," he said, "I wanted to play a special video made by our new friend, Jamie Sosa." Everyone clapped. Chip continued, "We lost Bianca's mother when Bianca was just a baby. I know that we are all wishing she could've been here to see her little girl all grown up, and I think, with this video, she can be, in a way."

A screen came down, and Jamie's video began. To the tune of Harry Belafonte's "Sweetheart from Venezuela," pictures of Binky and her mother flashed across the screen. Then came photos of Binky as a child interspersed with photos of her mother, Luz, as a child; photos of Binky in Miami; photos of her mother in Venezuela. All this led up to the final pairing: a video clip of Luz Mortimer in the Miss Universe contest, wearing her brilliant orange gown, and a video clip of Binky at Carmen's house, during the final fitting of her tangerine-colored dress. When the three-minute film was over, there wasn't a dry eye in the room.

"You're a girl of hidden talents," Bev Mortimer said, walking up to Jamie.

"Thanks," Jamie said, her heart beating quickly.

"Take good care of my stepson," Bev said. "I'm very fond of him."

"Me, too," Jamie said.

"Now, shouldn't you get back to work?" Bev asked, even though it was she who had come up to Jamie.

"Absolutely," Jamie said, happy to be offered the quick exit . . . and the praise.

After that, there was the father-daughter *vals*, and then the dance floor filled up once more. At the next lull in the music, Dash stood on a chair and tapped a glass. "Toast time! Toast time! But before we begin roasting and toasting my sister, a couple of my fellow *chambelanes* and I have prepared a little musical number for your entertainment."

Binky, who hadn't left Tino's side since the party began, sidled up to the girls of Amigas Inc. "You guys are too much."

Alicia raised two fingers. "*Amiga's* honor. We knew nothing about any number. This is a complete surprise to us, too."

They all watched, wondering what to expect, as Gaz, Domingo, Troy, and Dash took their places on the stage. They began singing an a capella number that they'd clearly written themselves. The lyrics were written to be sung to the tune of "How Do You Solve a Problem like Maria?" from Binky's all-time favorite movie, *The Sound of Music*:

> *How do you solve a problem like Bianca?*
> *How do you catch an heiress and pin her down?*
> *How do you find a word that means "Bianca"?*
> *A Wasp! A Latina! A quince on the town!*
>
> *She takes several hours in the bathroom*
> *Just to comb through all that silky hair;*
> *She waltzes like a linebacker in a scrimmage*
> *And salsas into every available chair.*
>
> *Oh, how do you solve a problem like Bianca?*
> *How do you breathe in the warmth of her embrace?*
> *How do you find a word that means Binky-Bianca?*
> *A birthday girl! A princess! A lady of taste!*

After the boys were done singing and taking multiple bows, Dash jumped off the stage and grabbed Jamie by the waist.

"When did you cook this up?" she asked him, laughing.

"Our business, not your business," Dash said mischievously. "Speaking of sneaky, how did you put together that amazing video?"

"That's an Amigas Inc. trade secret, my man," Jamie answered, her eyes sparkling with happiness. "My lips are sealed."

"I think I know a way to fix that, but I'll hold off until later. Are you ready to make your toast now?"

"Sure," she said, smoothing out her dress and running a hand through her hair nervously.

Dash grabbed a glass, tapped on it, and said, "*Damas y caballeros*, ladies and gentlemen: my beautiful girlfriend, Jamie Sosa."

Jamie, flushed, began, "I'm honored to be here tonight and honored that Bianca chose our company, Amigas Inc. (business cards are all over the ship, please call us!) to plan her *quinceañera*. As per tradition, we like to say something at each party we plan. So, first, I have to give a shout-out to my business partners and best friends, Alicia Cruz, Carmen Ramirez-Ruben, and

Gaspar Colón. And now, on to the birthday girl . . .

"Those of you who know Binky—I mean, Bianca—know that she's a hugger. I am not. When I first met B., her hugging completely freaked me out. But then, as I got to know more about Bianca and how young she was when she lost her mom, I realized that, more than most of us, Bianca understands that life can be cruel and short and therefore we should embrace it and grab all the hugs that we can. And I have to say, watching her transform into the girl you see tonight, she has got the embracing thing down. I never thought I'd say it, but, *chica*, you're a Latina, one hundred percent! So, if you could all please join me now in raising your glass to my new friend, Bianca. Come on up, *chica*!"

Binky got onstage and gave Jamie a huge hug, and then Jamie handed her the microphone.

"Thank you all for coming," Binky said, dabbing at her forehead with a handkerchief. "Is it me, or is it hot in here?" She unfolded a piece of paper and said, "Y'all know my Spanish is not the best. But tonight is all about honoring my Latina heritage, so I'm working on it, and I wanted to say a few words to you tonight *en español*:

"Toda mi vida, he sentido que me hace falta algo. Por supuesto que es mi mamá. Pero también mi cultura latina. Este día, con mi familia y mis amigos, siento que he recibido

esa parte de nuevo. Gracias. Y un gracias especial a Estrella.
Tu eres como una mamá para mi. Y siempre me recordó el
deseo de mi madre de tener mis quince.

"And now, in English:

"All of my life, I've felt like there was a part of me missing. Of course, part of that is missing my mother. But I've also missed my Latin culture. Today, with you—my family and friends—I feel like I've gotten back a little bit of what was missing. Thank you. And a special thanks to Estrella, who has been like a second mother to me and who reminded me, always, of my mother's desire to see me have my own *quinceañera*."

After Binky's speech, and after everyone who could had come and given her a hug and said congratulations, the birthday girl made her way over to the *amigas*. "May I see you for a moment?" she asked.

They all stepped to the side of the yacht, the waves crashing softly against the boat. All around them, people were smiling and dancing. It was a rare thing for the group to be able to take a moment and experience the joy that *quinceañeras* bring—especially in such a spectacular setting.

Binky handed Alicia an envelope. "This is a check."

Alicia looked confused. "But your father has already paid us."

"And tipped us," Carmen said.

"Very generously," Jamie added.

"This is a different check," Binky said. "It's a birthday gift from my father and Bev. This has been such an amazing experience for me. I'd like you to use this money to create another fabulous *quince* for a girl who can't afford one."

"Are you serious?" Carmen asked.

"Can we use your boat?" Jamie teased.

"You can't use my boat!" Binky said. "But you *can* have my money."

"This is amazing," Alicia said, giving Binky a hug. "It will make some girl very, very happy."

"One condition," Binky said, looking at Jamie. "I want to be anonymous. No game-show tactics this time."

"Done," Alicia said.

Just then, Tino approached the group. "Quit hogging my date!"

Binky turned to him and smiled. "I'm all yours." She gave the girls one last knowing look and then allowed herself to be led away to the dance floor.

For a moment, they all just stood there, transfixed. Jamie was about to go find Dash so that he could enjoy the moment, too, when Tilda Fales tapped her on the shoulder. "Are you girls hungry now?"

"Ravenous," Jamie said.

"Starved," Carmen added.

"Famished," chimed in Alicia.

"Well, then, follow me," Tilda said.

In the library of the ship, a room that they didn't even know existed, a small table had been set up with a white tablecloth, candles, and three place settings.

"Dinner is served," Tilda said with a grin, opening the door so the waiter could come in with the first course.

Over the candlelit meal, the members of Amigas sat down and began to replay the past five weeks, almost unable to process all that had happened in that short space of time.

"Can you believe that you *quit*?" Carmen said to Jamie.

"No way," said Jamie, chowing down on a plate of ceviche, guacamole, and homemade red tortilla chips. "I'm pretty sure you guys fired me."

"You quit," Alicia said.

"Whatever," Jamie said. "Details. Point is, I'm back."

"Better than ever," Carmen said.

"*Blonder* than ever," Alicia said.

Jamie blushed. "Oh, let it rest, it's just hair; it'll grow out."

"So, what does Dash think?" Carmen said, opening a bottle of sparkling apple cider.

"Did you see the way he can't take his eyes off of her?" Alicia said, waggling her eyebrows at Carmen. "I think he likes it."

"Can you believe it?" Jamie asked. "I have a boyfriend."

"We *all* have boyfriends," Alicia said.

"We'll have to do the double-date thing, but with all three couples," Carmen said, excitedly.

"You mean, triple-date?" Jamie asked.

"For some reason, that sounds so R-rated," Alicia said, giggling.

Just then, the *amigas* heard what sounded like an enormous explosion. Throwing their napkins and utensils down, they raced out onto the deck. They had each been trained in lifeboat evacuation, but none of them had ever actually expected to use it.

When they looked around, however, they saw that they were the only ones panicking. All of the other guests, crowded around the bow of the yacht, were staring up at the sky. The girls looked up and realized that the explosion they had heard was not a bomb but fireworks.

As the night exploded in color, their guys joined

them on the deck. Dash put his arm around Jamie. Gaz and Alicia held hands, and Domingo held Carmen close. Because this was a Mortimer *quince*, on a Mortimer yacht, for Chip Mortimer's only daughter, no ordinary fireworks would do. As the pink and orange and yellow streaks of light illuminated the sky, they spelled out words: *Feliz. Happy. Cumpleaños. Birthday. Querida Bianca. Dearest Bianca. Desea. Wish. Encima. Upon. Una estrella. A star.*

CHAPTER 21

FOR TWO WEEKS after Binky's event, Amigas Inc. posted the news of the free *quince* they were giving away on all the message boards they frequented. They put up signs all over Miami at their favorite spots, from Bongos to the empanada place. The sign said simply:

WIN A FREE *QUINCE*

A good Samaritan with a *corazón de oro* has donated a free *quince* to one deserving girl. Tell us in 300 words or less why you're the one. The lucky girl wins a *quince* worth $10,000, which includes limo service, a one-of-a-kind couture dress, an all-expenses-paid party for 50 guests, a $1,000 college scholarship, and the pro bono planning services of Amigas Inc.

Within days, the e-mails began to pour in; Alicia divvied them up between herself, Gaz, Carmen, and

Jamie for a first read. They quickly separated the applications into two piles: the frivolous and the fabulous.

The frivolous e-mails came from girls who wanted the *quince* money because they were too bratty to work with their parents' budget and/or rules. Sitting at Bongos, sipping on virgin *mojitos*, the crew gathered for a dramatic reading of their favorites from the "No Way, José" pile. Gaz and Alicia sat next to each other, holding hands underneath the table. Jamie sat in the center of the booth, looking fabulous with her dark blond hair. Carmen had taken a seat at the edge of the booth so she could steal quick kisses from Domingo, who was, as always, working.

Gaz picked up an e-mail and began to read in a high falsetto voice: *"I have always dreamed of a Versace quinceañera. . . ."*

"Does she mean a Versace dress?" Carmen asked. "Because my dresses are much, much better."

"Not to mention more *quince*-appropriate," Jamie added.

Gaz laughed, chowing down on yucca fries. "You have to hear the rest. *'I dream of a Versace-themed* quince *where I am an Italian princess, dripping in gold and swathed in silk.'"*

"Please, stop," Alicia begged.

"Are you kidding? Go on," Jamie said. "This is priceless."

Gaz continued reading. "*'My parents can't be my real parents because my real parents would understand the life of fabulosity that I crave. . . .'*"

"Maybe Binky should donate the money to *quinces* who need counseling, because this *chica* is a prime candidate," Carmen suggested.

Gaz held up a finger. "There's more. *'My parents don't support or understand my devotion to the House of Versace and how intricate the label is to my* quinceañera *plans.'*"

"I love fashion, but *ay*! It's too much," Carmen said.

"So shallow," Alicia said.

"So superficial," Jamie agreed. *"No más."*

While the pile of frivolous letters grew, so did the pile of fabulous ones. The girls heard from science-fair winners and Junior Olympics gymnasts. All in all, they received more than 300 applications and ended up with twenty-five finalists.

One Saturday afternoon, they met at Carmen's house to choose a winner. Binky and Tino were still dating, and she had been a regular presence at the Ramirez-Ruben household—despite the fact that she had once complained about how far the walk was from the parking lot.

Binky and Tino entered the living room both in jeans and nearly identical J. Crew T-shirts. Binky's was blue with a green collar, and Tino's was green with a blue collar.

"You dress alike now?" Carmen asked, amused.

"Don't be silly!" Binky said, even though it looked as though the idea were far from repulsive to her. "We went for a boat ride in the canal. Tino didn't want me to mess up my silk blouse, so he lent me this. Isn't that sweet? Okay if I wear this home?" she asked, turning to Tino.

Tino smiled. "You can keep it." He kissed her on the forehead. "Looks better on you than it does on me. I've gotta go to soccer practice. But I'll see you later for dinner, right?"

"Of course! The panini truck!" Binky cried. "I wouldn't miss it for the world. I'll text you when they tweet their location."

Although it had only been a couple of months, the girls were amazed by the transformation of their latest customer. *Quinceañeras* were funny that way. It was a ceremony designed to honor the young woman you were becoming—but with few exceptions, *planning* a *quince* was guaranteed to bring out your inner brat. If you got through it, however—the good and the bad, the stress and the strain, the ceremony and all the cultural richness—you always ended up a better person. *Sin falta.* Having planned more than a dozen *quinces* over the last year, the *amigas* had yet to met a girl who didn't experience a big growing-up arc in the process. Which is why their latest business cards read:

AMIGAS INC.

Once-in-a-lifetime *quinces*.
Because it's so much
more than a party.

Binky took a seat on the sofa next to Jamie. Gaz and Alicia sat cross-legged on the floor, and Carmen nipped in and out—first to get a pitcher of fruit punch, then to bring in a plate of pumpkin empanadas.

"So, Binky," Alicia said, pointing to the stack of e-mails on the coffee table. "We received more than three hundred applications in all."

"Wow, that's great!" Binky squealed.

"Not as great as these empanadas," Gaz said, shoveling one into his mouth.

Alicia swatted him on the shoulder. "Focus, hungry man." Then she turned to Binky. "After an exhaustive process, we've narrowed them down to twenty-five, and because you're the one giving away this *quince*, we thought you should pick the winner."

Binky's eyes grew wide. "Wow. Big responsibility."

"You can do it," Jamie said. "Just picture yourself chilling with those girls at the Luz Invitational. Who would you like to see have the *quince* of her dreams?"

Alicia handed her the stack of e-mails and they all sat quietly as she read through each one. The canal glistened behind her, and the little Venice-style footbridges absorbed the bright Miami light.

"This girl wants to be a doctor and go to Harvard," Binky said, sounding impressed.

"That's Carolina; she's my pick," Gaz said. "Choose her."

"No campaigning!" Carmen said, throwing a pillow at Gaz.

"This girl wants to be an artist and dreams of having a Tina Modotti *quince*," Binky said.

"Michelle, my girl," Jamie called out.

"No campaigning!" Alicia and Carmen said, in unison.

"There's so many deserving girls," Binky said quietly. "How can I choose just one?"

She returned to the stack, and as she began reading

the next entry, her eyes filled with tears. "This is the one," she said.

"Is it Zoe?" Carmen asked, forgetting her own rule. "She's my favorite."

Binky nodded and read the application essay out loud.

> My name is Zoe Herrera and I'm fourteen years old. I live with my dad in Pembroke Pines. Every year since I was a baby, my mother bought a hundred-dollar savings bond toward my *quinceañera*. She passed away when I was ten years old. I've got ten savings bonds worth a thousand dollars so I wouldn't need the full award. You can donate the rest to charity. My birthday is February 13th and my dream is to have a Valentine's Day *quince* at the Roll Bounce skating rink here in Pembroke Pines. It's the place where my parents met.

Binky's voice cracked as she read the letter. There was no doubt. Zoe Herrera would make a fine winner.

Alicia handed her the phone. "You call her and give her the good news."

Binky shook her head. "No way; I want to be completely anonymous."

"It's just a phone call," Alicia said. "Pretend to be me."

Binky grinned and took the phone. "Okay. That works." She dialed the number and, putting on a posh accent, said, "Good afternoon. May I speak to Zoe Herrera?" She put her hand over the phone and whispered, "They are going to get her.

"Hello, darling," Binky purred as she resumed speaking into the phone. "This is Alicia Cruz, *presidente, jefe,* chief, and general of Amigas Inc."

Carmen, Gaz, and Jamie could hardly contain their guffaws. Alicia, pretending to be miffed, protested, "Hey, I'm not that bad!"

"I'm delighted to tell you that you are the winner of an all-expenses-paid *quinceañera* and a one-thousand-dollar college scholarship." She held the phone away from her ear, and all of the others could hear Zoe Herrera screaming, *"Ay, Dios mio! Ay, Dios mio!"*

Binky giggled. "I'd say she's pleased," she said in a whisper to the team. "Listen, darling," she continued, resuming the posh accent, "my people will call your people."

She waited as Zoe asked a question and then said, "Your people is really your dad. We'll call him."

She paused again and then spoke with no accent at all. "You're so welcome. Congratulations, Zoe. I know your mother would be very proud."

EPILOGUE

TWO MONTHS LATER, all of the members of Amigas Inc. gathered on the balcony of the Roll Bounce skating rink. Gaz stood behind Alicia, his arms draped around her shoulders. Carmen put her arm around Jamie, who had her arm, in turn, around their honorary guest, Binky Mortimer.

They watched the action in the rink below them. Zoe Herrera and her father were doing their father-daughter *vals*—on roller skates.

"I love *quinces*," Alicia said.

"Sometimes I think about the time when I'll be too old to be a *quince* guest," Carmen said. "It's going to be sad, like being too old to play with dolls."

"I think we have a ways to go before we're too old to come to *quinces*," Binky said.

Watching Zoe and her father skate arm in arm, Jamie said, "Look at how happy Zoe is. You did good, B."

Binky smiled. "I provided the check, but you *chicas* did all of the hard work. The way I see it, we *all* did good."

"Are you sure you don't want to meet her?" Alicia asked.

Binky shook her head. "I like being the anonymous donor," she said. "I just wanted to see her in her dress, dancing the father-daughter *vals*. Now that I've seen it, I've got to go. Tino's got a big game tonight."

She hugged each of the members of Amigas Inc. Then she left through the back door, without Zoe Herrera's ever knowing that her fairy godmother had been there—at her ball. It was a strange but wonderful world in which Amigas Inc. existed. A world where four fifteen-year-olds could run the hottest *quince* planning business in town. A world where a fairy godmother could wear skinny jeans and patent-leather pumps and be too young to drive. And a world where a girl could skate her way into being fifteen, both literally and figuratively. Only in Miami, *chicas*. Only in Miami.

A Chat With
Jennifer Lopez

When I first came up with the idea for the Amigas *series, I thought about the many Latina women who, like Alicia, Jamie, and Carmen, had started out as entrepreneurial teenagers. Who, through hard work, imagination, and dedication, were able to take their passions and talents and become role models and successful adults. For me, Jennifer Lopez is such a woman. She has incredible drive and an amazing work ethic, qualities she shares with the girls in* Amigas. *They, too, needed an equal amount of determination to turn their* quince-party-planning *business into a huge success.*

So, to get a better sense of this connection, I sat down with Jennifer, and we talked about quinces *and what it was like for her as a Latina girl growing up in New York City. Here are some more of her answers. . . .*

—J. Startz

1. Jamie takes center stage in *She's Got Game*. Like you, Jamie is a young woman who grew up in the Bronx. What do you remember as being the most fun about growing up in the Bronx? Were there any challenges?

Growing up in the Bronx was a great experience for me. Like many neighborhoods in New York, the Bronx has a great sense of family, community, and arts as well. I used to dance at various centers in the neighborhood. I fondly remember that when it came time to name my first album, I chose On the 6, because that was the subway train I would take into Manhattan from the Bronx.

2. For someone so young, Jamie seems to be her own person and to have a really strong sense of self. Do you recognize any of yourself in Jamie? If so, in what ways are you similar? In what ways are you different?

Jamie and I are both motivated and focused. We also have a huge passion for shoes! (Jamie's love for sneakers is much like my love for shoes and boots.) I think Jamie's tough exterior can sometimes be misunderstood, and I can relate to that.

3. Jamie goes through a few changes in her style in this book, and some of her choices (wrongly or rightly) are influenced by the people with whom she is socializing. From where did you draw your fashion inspiration? Looking back, did you make any big fashion faux pas as a young woman?

I love to play with fashion, mixing up styles. But the most important thing is to wear what makes you feel good, not what is trendy. I also love flipping through magazines for inspiration, like most girls! I think we all have some fashion no-no's, and I bet mine are out there somewhere. ☺

4. Jamie reacts very strongly to Dash's stepmom's snobbery and judgmental nature. As a public figure who has had to learn how to navigate the tricky waters of celebrity, what advice would you give to young women who are worried or concerned about being judged and living up to other people's standards?

Thankfully, I had a lot of love and support from my family, which gave me confidence at a young age. I would advise young girls this way—hold your head high, and always believe in yourself.

5. Jamie starts out in the story prejudging Binky. Have you ever had any girlfriends that have surprised you— the same way that Jamie sort of didn't expect to like Binky and then wound up embracing her as a friend?

Most of my girlfriends I've known for a long time, but every now and then you meet people you may be unsure about at first. The key is to not judge anyone right off the bat, because you never know; Jamie definitely learns that lesson with Binky.

6. What strengths have you drawn from your family and your Latina heritage that have helped you to accomplish what you've wanted to do?

Latin people are very warm and family-oriented. I have a lot of women in my family between my sisters and cousins—we're like older amigas! My family has so many wonderful qualities that have helped guide me along the way. My passion and work ethic definitely come from my parents.

Make sure to RSVP for the next quinceañera!

Amigas
Playing for Keeps

by Veronica Chambers

Created by Jane Startz
Inspired by Jennifer Lopez

CHAPTER 1

FIFTEEN-YEAR-OLD Alicia Cruz did not start her *quinceañera* planning business to be popular. As the wealthy and beautiful daughter of one of Miami's most prominent power couples, she'd never lacked for friends. But ever since Alicia, along with her best friends—Carmen Ramirez-Ruben, Jamie Sosa, and Gaz Colón (who was now Alicia's boyfriend as well)—had formed Amigas Incorporated and in the process planned more than twenty of the hottest Sweet Fifteen parties in the greater Miami area, her profile at Coral Gables High School had never been higher.

Every afternoon, when the four friends sat at their table in the school cafeteria—second from the right, near the sliding doors, with floor-to-ceiling views of the school's lush, tropical campus—they were flooded with visits from C. G. High students hoping to get a little free *quince* advice.

On this particular Thursday, Alicia, Carmen, and Jamie had just sat down to eat a lunch supplied by Maribelle Puentes, the Cruz family cook and Alicia's de facto grandmother. Maribelle had recently started dating Tomas, a Peruvian-Japanese chef from the trendy restaurant Nobu Miami, and in honor of him had added sushi-making to her repertoire of already impressive culinary skills.

Alicia handed both of her friends a small tin *bento* box, professionally packed in an insulated bag.

"Maribelle wanted you guys to try some, too," Alicia explained, opening her lunchbox to reveal twelve perfect, restaurant-quality Japanese sushi rolls. "I'm in heaven," she sighed. "Yellowtail scallion rolls."

"Spicy shrimp tempura hand rolls, my favorite," Jamie said, tucking in to her sushi.

Carmen, who'd already popped a bite of tuna tataki into her mouth, pointed to her face and offered a thumbs-up. "*Chicas,*" she sighed contentedly when she finished chewing, "I truly don't think our lives could get any better than this—sunny weather, yummy food, and hot boyfriends. How cool is it that?"

She wasn't lying. Her hot boyfriend was Domingo Quintero, a senior at Hialeah High and a waiter at Bongos, the group's favorite restaurant, famous for its frequent celebrity sightings and delicious virgin *mojitos*. Not only was he super good-looking, he also happened to be supernice.

Earlier that year, Jamie had started dating Dash Mortimer, a golf star who happened to be heir to a considerable fortune. Dash was not your typical Latin guy, which had caused some issues when he first showed interest in hotheaded Jamie. His late mom had been a Venezuelan beauty queen, and his father traced his family's lineage back to the *Mayflower*. Amigas Inc. had been hired to plan a *quince* for Binky, Dash's socialite sister, which was how he had met Jamie. They both fell hard. A fierce salsa dancer, Dash moved with the confidence of a gifted athlete, and had been the only guy to break down the tough-girl exterior Jamie had rocked since she'd moved to Miami from the Bronx.

"Speaking of boyfriends, I wish Gaz was here," Alicia said with a sigh.

Alicia and Gaz—an aspiring musician, a founding member of Amigas Inc., and formerly one of Alicia's best friends—had been officially dating now for about a year. "You know how obsessed he is with sushi," she added, "not to mention Maribelle's cooking. My bet is that he's still in the music room, working on some new songs."

Unfortunately, talk about boyfriends was going to have to be put on hold, because it appeared someone needed their help. The someone was a classmate of theirs, a boy named Nesto.

"Sorry to interrupt," he said, coming to stand at the head of their table. "I just have a quick question. This girl I really like, Tia, asked me to be her *chambelán de honor* at her *quinceañera*."

"That sounds great," Jamie said, causing both Alicia and Carmen to smile. Since Jamie had started dating Dash, she had become more comfortable showing her softer side—a welcome change for her two best friends, who in the past had often found themselves apologizing to their clients for their friend's extreme bluntness and occasionally acid tongue.

"Congrats," Carmen mumbled, since he'd caught her in midchew.

"Thanks. I can't wait," he said. "It's not an Amigas Inc. joint, but it should be a good party all the same."

"So, how can we help?" Alicia asked, getting right to the point.

"I really like this girl," Nesto said. "But I've got about fifty dollars to get her a *quince* present. All my boys say you've got to drop at least a C-note for something nice."

"Not true," Jamie said.

"Not at all," Alicia agreed, finishing up her last piece of sushi.

"Well, I went to the Gap. . . ." Nesto said.

"Not the Gap!" cried Carmen.

"Why not?" asked Nesto, perplexed.

"Never the Gap for a *quince*!" Jamie piped in. "That's where you go to buy your back-to-school clothes, not the special something for the girl of your dreams. You know what *would* be perfect?"

Nesto shrugged. "I don't. That's why I came to you guys."

"A charm bracelet," Alicia said.

"Silver," Carmen added.

Jamie took out a card and said, "Go to Key and Ree. Ask for Josefina. She'll help you pick out something nice."

"And there's a ten percent discount for Amigas Inc. clients," Alicia added. "Tell her we sent you."

Nesto was all smiles as he glanced down at the card and then back at them. "You guys are the best."

"Glad we could help," Alicia said.

But there was no rest for the weary. As soon as Nesto walked away, a girl named Liya ran up to their table.

"Hey, I know I'm not one of your clients, but I could really use some advice," she said.

Alicia looked at her watch. "We've got a few more minutes. What's up?"

"I'm having a Nancy Drew *quince*," Liya said.

The girls exchanged curious and amused glances.

"Yeah, I'm really excited. We're doing a whole murder-mystery game thing. And I need to figure out some favors for one hundred people. And needless to say, I'm on a budget, or I would have totally hired you guys."

"Hmm, a Nancy Drew–themed favor," Alicia said. "That's a tough one."

She took out her phone and started searching for some options. Thirty seconds later, she had an answer.

"This Web site has a free Nancy Drew bookmark you can download," Alicia said.

"Then go and get them printed and laminated," Jamie added.

"Don't forget to put a picture of you in your *quince* dress on the back," Carmen suggested.

"If you have the loot, you could punch a hole in the top and tie a ribbon and add a little chain with your initials," Jamie said.

Once the *amigas* started giving *quince* advice, even pro bono, it was hard for them to stop.

"Perfect!" Liya said, her eyes lighting up. "I'll order

them tonight. I would never have thought of this. You rock!"

"We aim to please," Alicia said.

"You know, the potential for our business really is limitless," Jamie said when they were once again blissfully alone. "We could make some sort of discount-coupon book for all the great deals we get around town."

"I'm already getting a commercial discount at the fabric store," Carmen said.

Jamie held up her thumb and index finger and said, "We're *this close* to having a *quince* empire."

As the friends laughed, the bell rang. Grabbing her books, Alicia said, "And I'm *this* close to failing organic chemistry. I love being the queen of *quince*, but it's a full-time job."

"*Ay*, don't mention the word *fail*," Carmen said. "I wanted to go to the library to research traditional Mexican costumes for dress ideas. But I've got to use my study hall to write a draft of my American history paper. See you *chicas* later."

Carmen gave her girls a quick hug and took off down the south hallway. Like many historic buildings in South Florida, C. G. High was a one-story art deco building with big windows, white walls, and large open spaces.

The halls were lined with brightly lit display cases. Some were filled with trophies won by the school's varsity football team, the Cavaliers. Others featured writing and artwork from the senior literary magazine, *Catharsis*, or solicitations for donations for school supplies for C.G.'s sister school in the Dominican Republic.

"I'm going to life drawing, so I'll walk you to the science class," Jamie said to Alicia.

As the girls made their way down the hall they were greeted by other students.

"Nice party last weekend," a girl with red hair called out.

"Thanks," Alicia and Jamie said in unison.

"Yo, Gaz said he'd burn me a CD of those tracks he played at Katerina's *quince*," a boy in a C.G. letter jacket called out. "Tell him it's for Gary."

"I will," Alicia said.

Jamie grinned. "It's kind of cool, isn't it?"

"What?"

"It's like we're famous," Jamie said.

A group of girls who had attended Carmen's multi-culti "Lati-Jew-na" *quince* honoring her mixed Jewish and Latino heritage walked by and held up the spray-painted bags that Jamie had made for their best friend's celebration. "*Hola y* shalom," the girls called out, using the Spanish and Hebrew words for *hello* that Jamie had tagged in block-print graffiti on the front and back of each guest's stylish party favor. Jamie laughed. "You see what I mean?"

Alicia had to agree. In their corner of the world, there was no doubt they really were almost famous. Life, it would seem, couldn't get much sweeter.

To be continued ...